Trouble in Masai Mara

Books by Maylan Schurch:

Justin Case Adventures:

1. *The Case of the Stolen Red Mary*
2. *The Desert Temple Mystery*
3. *Danger Signals in Belize*

Beware of the Crystal Dragon

Blinded by the Light

The Great Graffiti Mystery

The Rapture

Rescue From Beyond Orion

A Thousand Shall Fall

Trouble in Masai Mara

MAYLAN SCHURCH

REVIEW AND HERALD® PUBLISHING ASSOCIATION
HAGERSTOWN, MD 21740

The author assumes full responsibility for the accuracy of all facts and quotations as cited in this book.

This book was
Edited by Randy Fishell
Designed by Tina Ivany
Electronic makeup by Toya M. Koch
Cover illustration by Del Thompson/Thompson Brothers
Typeset: Cheltenham Book 11/16

PRINTED IN U.S.A.

06 05 04 03 02 5 4 3 2 1

R&H Cataloging Service
Schurch, Maylan Henry, 1950-
Trouble in Masai Mara.

I. Title.

813.6

ISBN 0-8280-1614-3

Dedication

This book is dedicated to the memory of my junior teachers,
Lois and Merlin Anderson,
who treated us with great dignity.

Acknowledgments

A big thank-you to my fellow pastor, Ron Preast, who made available to me 2,200 digital photos from the Kenya adventure he led in the spring of 2001. The Kirkland Seventh-day Adventist Church, along with a small army of teens and adults, held an evangelistic series and a Vacation Bible School while building a worship and training center in just eight days.

And, as always, warm thanks to Randy Fishell, who edits both *Guide* magazine and the Justin Case series, and who also has a small army (of sons) who keeps him straight on what kids really like to read. He then passes this information on to me, and I follow it as best I can.

* * * * *

Contents

Surprise Time in Nairobi

The adventure that would give Justin Case great memories forever—and nightmares for about a week—began quite calmly in the back seat of a taxi in Nairobi, Kenya.

"Jambo," said Robert Case to his son, poking him in the ribs with his *Traveler's Companion* guidebook.

The Kenyan taxi driver in the front seat glanced quickly around and grinned. *"Jambo, bwana."*

"Sorry," Mr. Case said to him. "I'm coaching my son in Swahili. We're learning together."

The driver's grin widened. "It is a very easy language."

"Hear that, Justin? Swahili's easy. *Jambo."*

"Jambo, baba," Justin said in an absent-minded voice, staring ahead down the street.

"Baba?" Dad flipped hastily through the *Traveler's Companion.* "It's hard to concentrate riding in a Nairobi taxi. What's *baba?"*

"'Father,'" Justin translated.

"Looks as though you got to this book before I did."

Justin nodded. "Dad, look. What's that?"

"What's what?"

"Up ahead, in the next block. Those big white pointy things curving up over the street. They look like humongous elephant tusks."

The driver chuckled. "Yes! They are elephant tusks!"

"They *can't* be." Justin fumbled in his belt pack and brought out something that looked like half a binocular. "They're like 30 feet long!"

"Fifty, easy," Dad said solemnly.

The driver's voice became equally solemn. "Kenya have big elephants. *Beeeeg* elephants."

"Must have taken a pretty good-sized rifle to get that one," Dad said.

"British army cannon," the driver murmured reverently. "Boom!"

"We'll have to be careful when we go on safari later this week," Dad said with mock concern.

Justin squinted through his scope and focused it. "They're fake!" he announced.

The driver laughed even louder than before. "No, no! Beeeeg elephant!"

Dad poked his son again. "We gotcha!"

"I knew they weren't real." Justin craned his neck and stared up at the huge tusks as the taxi passed beneath them. They were planted in the ground on both sides of the road, and arched up to cross in the middle.

"Reminds me of when I was a kid," Dad said, "when the circus came to town. I liked the elephants most of all. They're so huge and powerful, yet they can be controlled by a human being. For almost two years I wanted to be an elephant trainer." He tapped the large digital camera hanging around his neck. "I'm going to get as close as I can to them on the safari, and take lots of pictures."

He stared out the window of the taxi. The day was bright and sunny, but not too hot. They were passing a large Muslim mosque that had white domes and two tall gray towers. In front of it was a courtyard covered with large pieces of striped cloth supported by poles. Underneath, hundreds of Muslims were bowing in prayer. "Look at all those people," Dad said. "Driver, what's the population of Nairobi?"

"Two million. Maybe more."

"So how," Justin asked, "are we going to find Monique?"

"Easy . . . I hope." Dad opened to a map in the *Traveler's Companion* that he'd marked with a paper clip. He put his finger down on the page. "We're here. Now, do you see this blank spot up here?" Dad asked, moving his finger to another location on the map. "Someone built a new horse-racing track there, newer even than this book. And not too far from it is a shantytown."

"What's a shantytown?"

"It's a town of shacks. Sort of a slum. Kenya has a lot of unemployed people, because the economy's really bad, and a lot of folks just live there in the shacks trying to find work in town. The Walters have set up their dental clinic there for a few weeks." Dad suddenly grinned. "I can't wait to see Monique's expression when she spots you."

"Are you sure she doesn't know I'm coming?"

"Jerry and Lucinda promised to keep it a secret."

They rode along in silence for a while. Justin decided that Nairobi looked pretty much like any other big city, and he was getting bored. He unzipped his belt pack and saw his CD player. And he thought about Shannon.

"Dad?"

"What?"

"Do you have any double-A batteries?"

"None to spare."

"Could we get some?"

Dad glanced down at the belt pack and then stared at his son. "You brought your CD player with you?"

"Sure."

"This may be the only chance you ever have to explore Africa, and you bring a *CD player?"*

Justin didn't say anything but stared out the window at a huge fresh fruit market. Women in colorful robes smiled and laughed with each other.

"Look, I want this to be a fun trip for you," Dad said. "So I'm not going to go into my lecture mode. But can't you get along without that thing for even a minute? Did you take it with you when you went with Rico to Belize?"

Justin shook his head.

"And you didn't miss it, right?"

"Not really."

"Justin, in the next few days you're going to see things that the singers on those CDs of yours will never see. Not even Sally Ferguson."

"Her name's Shannon," Justin growled.

"Whatever," Dad said. *"Shannon* Ferguson. But just the same—"

"Shannon *Fagin,"* Justin interrupted. "She's Irish."

Dad eyed him thoughtfully. "Well, whoever she is, she's got you in her grip. What is it about her music you like? The beat? The animal howls?"

"Dad, Shannon Fagin is a Christian. She sings *Christian* songs."

"Well, that's good." Dad glanced at the driver, then bent his head close to his son and lowered his voice. "But think about *this*. Kenya can be a dangerous place if you're young and defenseless." He held up the *Traveler's Companion* and wiggled it in Justin's face. "Every few pages, this book reminds visitors to watch out for bandits. And if a 12-year-old tourist goes strolling around with earphone cords hanging from his ears, somebody'll want to steal what's on the other end of those cords. And the next thing you know, you'll be lying in some back alley, with—"

"OK," Justin said, "forget the batteries."

"Hey, guy," Dad said sympathetically, "I only want you to be safe. And to take full advantage of this trip, that's all. Like the safari."

"I know."

While they were speaking, the taxi driver was swooping down street after street, honking at bicyclists or anybody else in his way. Finally the buildings got smaller and farther apart. At the very edge of the city the driver pulled up in front of a huge sea of tin and wood and canvas shacks. The driver turned his head anxiously and spoke to Mr. Case.

"You want to go *here?*" he asked.

"Just drive along slowly," Dad said. "I'm looking for a brand-new silver Land Rover."

The driver's eyes widened, as if somebody had told him the arched elephant tusks were genuine after all. "A *new* Land Rover? *Here?"*

Dad nodded. "With a white tent beside it."

"Look, a soccer game!" Justin said suddenly. About a dozen boys, a couple of them wearing very little clothing, pursued a tired old volleyball down a winding side street.

"Not one of those kids gets one decent meal a week, I'll bet," Dad said sadly.

"Land Rover!" the driver called out. "Over there."

Dad glanced at where the driver was pointing. "Yes, that looks like the one Jerry described." He stared around at the shacks, and then down at the camera around his neck. "Better get us as close as you can."

"Yes, *bwana."*

After they'd stopped, Dad paid the driver. As the taxi drove away, Justin and his father began threading their way through the shacks toward the Land Rover. Immediately they were surrounded by about 30 little children, who stared up at them.

"We'd better get a suntan, quick," Dad whispered. "Everybody here knows that White people without suntans are tourists." He grinned.

Although there was a long line of Kenyans waiting outside the tent, Justin didn't see his friend Monique or her parents until he slipped up beside the tent and peeked inside.

Two patients sat in folding chairs, and Monique's dentist parents, Jerry and Lucinda Walters, were each hovering over one of the chairs. Monique, seated on a little stool beside the woman her dad was working on, held a crying baby.

The patient gave a quick gasp.

"There!" Dr. Walters said cheerfully, though Justin noticed that the man's voice sounded weary. "Came out nice and clean. That tooth won't bother you any more, mama. Monique, give her a baby health kit too."

The woman stood up, smiling with relief. She reached into a bag that hung around her neck with a string. *"Ngapi?"*

"Hapana," Monique replied expertly. "There is no charge. Here's your baby, and I'll get you some baby supplies."

"Asante sana," the woman said over and over, thanking Dr. Walters and Monique. As the woman clutched her infant, Justin saw tears in her eyes—from pain or from gratitude, he wasn't sure. When Monique's back was turned, Justin quickly stepped forward.

She turned back and spotted him.

At first she gave Justin a single curious glance and gave the baby kit to the mother. But then she swiveled sharply around again. Her eyes had gone huge, and her jaw sagged. For five whole seconds she froze. Then one of her hands crept out to touch him.

"Justin?" she shrieked.

He grinned. "Knock-knock."

"Where did—what are you—how did you *get* here?" she gasped.

"Knock-knock."

"Mom! Dad!" she whirled to face them. "Justin's here!" Then she saw their smiles. "You knew! You knew it all along!"

"Knock-knock," Justin patiently repeated.

"Didn't you leave those jokes of yours back in America?" Monique asked in a dazed voice. "OK—who's there?"

"Kenya."

"Kenya who?"

He grinned. "Kenya believe I'm here?"

She gave him a quick impulsive hug. "Wow! Oh, this is *awesome!*"

"Monique," Lucinda Walters said, "why don't you show Justin around a little? Don't go too far."

"Sure, Mom." Monique led Justin through a curtain into the other half of the tent. "You sneak," she said, staring at him. "How long have you been here?"

"We flew in this afternoon." Justin sighed. "And we've got bad news for your mom and dad."

She frowned. "The medical supplies."

Justin nodded. "Mr. Frazier's doing the best he can, but they're not going to get here till sometime next week. Sorry."

She sighed, her hand on the outside tent flap. Then she turned back. "Let's not go outside yet," she said. "Unless you want a billion little kids hanging around you. I have been *so* homesick," she sighed. "Even for you and those lame jokes of yours. What are you guys doing down here, anyway?"

"Mr. Frazier paid our way."

"Just to make sure we got those supplies he's donating?"

Justin nodded. "That too. But he also wants us to scout out other medical teams who can really use his help. Dad's going to write articles about the trip too."

"Mr. Frazier's video game business must be doing well."

He nodded. "And his Herod's Temple exhibit in Arizona is really popular. So he's got money to spare."

"Cool." She sighed. "But Mom and Dad are going to be really disappointed about those supplies. Did you see that baby kit I gave out? I think we've got just four more."

"So your parents are doing more than just dental work?"

Monique nodded her head. "People have all sorts of problems. So Mom and Dad are doing a lot of medical clinic stuff too—sewing stitches, giving antibiotics, that kind of thing. And they didn't come prepared with a lot of those types of supplies. They've been able to get some things locally, but those places are running out now. This is a really poor country."

Monique rolled her shoulders to take out the aches. "I'm glad we're starting on that safari the day after tomorrow. Mom and Dad really need a break." Suddenly she looked at him. "Why don't you and your dad come along?"

Justin grinned. "We are!"

"This is so great!" Monique said. She gazed at him again and sighed. "I've been here only two weeks, and it's like I've been gone a year. What's happening back home? How's Rico?"

"Great. He and I spent some time in Belize with his uncle."

"I know. You headed down there just before my folks got me my Africa ticket. Any new music back home?"

"Shannon Fagin's got a new one—'Green Fields of Grace.'"

"Did you bring it along?"

“Right here.” Justin patted his belt pack, and lowered his voice. “But Dad’s all growly because I brought along my player. He thinks I should concentrate on Africa.”

“ ‘Green Fields of Grace’? Is it good? Let me listen.”

“Sure.” He unzipped the pack and took out the CD player with its earbud cords and handed it to her. “It’s on track 5, but it might cut out on you. The batteries are low, and Dad won’t let me get new ones.”

“I’d lend you some, but mine died already. Batteries cost a lot here.” She inserted the earbuds and began pushing buttons on the player.

While she listened, humming once in awhile, Justin cautiously cracked the back tent flap and peered outside at the low shacks. *How can anybody live in those?* he wondered.

Suddenly a tuneful *plunk-plunk-plunkity-plunk* sounded from back behind the curtain, over in the medical clinic half.

“What’s that noise?” he asked Monique.

Her eyes widened. Clicking the STOP on the CD player, she bundled its cords around it and thrust it into his hands.

“Hide this, quick,” she said. “Isaiah’s here.”

The Racetrack

"Who's Isaiah?" Justin asked, juggling the CD player in one hand while struggling with the belt pack zipper with the other.

Monique put her finger to her lips.

The curtain opened, and a smiling young Kenyan appeared. In a single swooping glance he took in Monique and Justin. And the CD player.

"Hello," he said.

"Hi, Isaiah," Monique said. "This is my friend Justin Case. He just got here from America. Justin, this is Isaiah Kwendo."

Isaiah's smile widened. "My pleasure," he said, extending his hand. He seemed to be about their age—13, give or take a few months, and wore a red T-shirt, khaki shorts, and leather sandals. Hanging around his neck was a bright-red wooden box about the size of a fat paperback book. Fanned across its top was a cluster of thin, flat pieces of metal.

Isaiah saw Justin staring at the box and grinned. "Thumb piano," he said. "My own 'CD player.'" He started plunking out a happy tune with many intertwining rhythms. Then he stopped, held out the box, and glanced at the CD player. "Want to trade?"

Justin smiled and shook his head.

Isaiah dangled the red box invitingly. “Have you ever seen one of these before?”

Justin shook his head.

“You will never make a trade like this again,” Isaiah said. “You cannot buy this thumb piano in America. But I could buy your CD player in Nairobi.”

“If you had the money,” Monique spoke up.

Isaiah laughed. “That is the problem. No mon-neee.”

“Isaiah,” said a deep male voice from the other side of the curtain. “Where are you?”

“Bother,” Isaiah muttered softly. “I have to go to work.”

“Where do you work?” Justin asked.

“The Uhuru Riding Club, next to the racetrack near here.”

Monique flickered her eyelashes. “You’re lucky. All those beautiful horses.”

“Justin, come see where I work,” Isaiah invited. “Monique has been there.”

Monique brightened and nodded. “Let’s go ask permission.”

Justin stuffed his CD player into his belt pack, and they rejoined his dad and Monique’s parents. Justin was introduced to Joseph Kwendo, a handsome, muscular, uniformed man who stood straight like a soldier. After several cautious questions, Robert Case’s face relaxed, and he gave permission for his son to go.

“It will be for just two hours,” Mr. Kwendo said. “I will drop them off there and come back here. I want to talk to you, Mr. Case.”

Joseph Kwendo led the three young people to an ancient vehicle that looked a little like a roofless army jeep, and soon they were on their way.

"I am so glad that you and your father have come to Kenya, Justin," Mr. Kwendo said in his pleasant bass voice. "Monique's father has told me about how your father was once a police officer. I have been hoping to ask him some questions."

"Are you a police officer too?" Justin asked.

Mr. Kwendo shook his head. "No, I am a park ranger."

"It is sometimes the same thing, *baba,*" Isaiah said.

"Indeed," his father agreed. "One of my responsibilities is to help prevent poaching."

Justin gave a puzzled frown. "You mean it's against the law to boil eggs in Kenya?"

Mr. Kwendo laughed. "No, that is a different type of poaching. This type of poaching involves shooting animals illegally. Such as elephants."

"Why," Justin asked, "would anybody want to shoot an elephant?"

"For the ivory," said Isaiah.

Mr. Kwendo nodded. "Poachers often shoot elephants, then saw off the tusks and carry them away and sell them, leaving the animals to decay in the sun."

"That's terrible," Monique said. "But poaching is against the law, right?"

"That is correct," Mr. Kwendo said. "And the government has now adopted a shoot-to-kill policy. Poachers now take their own lives in their hands."

"Whoa." Justin shuddered. "So if people know they might be shot, why do they still try to poach?"

Mr. Kwendo shrugged. "Our country is large," he said, "and the antipoaching units cannot be everywhere at once. Some people will take big risks for big money."

A moment later Mr. Kwendo pulled up at the entrance to the Uhuru Riding Club, a white barnlike building near a large pasture surrounded by a white wooden fence. "I will be back at 6:00," he said, and the jeep sputtered away toward the shantytown again.

"Do you like horses?" Isaiah asked Justin. "I know Monique does."

Justin shrugged. "Last week I was a little hoarse myself."

Isaiah bent his head politely forward. "What did you say?"

"When I had a cold."

"Ignore him, Isaiah," Monique said firmly. "Justin likes to think he's a comedian. Don't encourage him."

"H-o-r-s-e and h-o-a-r-s-e," Justin spelled helpfully. "It was a joke."

Isaiah smiled and said a polite "Ha, ha." Then he glanced at his watch. "I must report to the office for my work duties. Monique, you know where the saddles are kept. Brownie and Ralph need some exercise. Brownie would be best for Justin if he is not used to riding." He jogged off in the direction of a small white building attached to the barn.

"I think I'll just watch," Justin said.

"Oh, no, you don't," Monique said. "Brownie's a sweetie. Haven't you been on a horse before?"

"Well, no." Justin waved her away. "But you go ahead. I'll be OK."

"Follow me," Monique commanded. "Or maybe you're too scared."

Justin sighed, and followed her. "But wait," he said. "What's Isaiah's boss going to say?"

"It's fine. These older horses need exercise, but nobody rides them much because they're so slow. All we'll do is get on them and walk them around the yard. Maybe trot a little too."

"What if I get bucked off?"

"Brownie doesn't have a single buck to his name," the girl insisted.

"Like Isaiah?"

"What?" She stared at him suspiciously. "Oh. Bucks. *Money.*" She snorted. "Let's just hope Brownie doesn't mind your weird jokes. They say horses can smell fear. Maybe they can smell bad jokes too."

When she saddled the small brown horse and brought him over, Justin got around in front of Brownie and stared at him.

"What are you doing?" his friend asked.

"Trying to get some insight into his personality."

Monique examined the horse thoughtfully. "I don't think he has one," she said. "Or maybe he's just asleep. Don't be afraid of him. Just get on."

Justin put a foot in the stirrup and started to ascend. Monique let him get halfway up before she spoke.

"Wrong foot," she said. "If you go all the way, you'll be

facing Brownie's backside. Not a great view."

"Whoops." He cautiously lowered himself to the ground again. This time he got the correct foot in the stirrup, but when he was halfway up Brownie started to move impatiently. Only by sheer luck did Justin land in the saddle, and he did so with a jolt.

"Ouch!" he cried out.

"Don't yank the reins," Monique warned him. "Just be gentle. How would you like to have a metal bar between *your* teeth?"

"Maybe I should get off right now and spare Brownie all this pain," he said hopefully.

"You stay up there," Monique commanded.

"He probably wants to be back in his stall eating . . . uh, eating whatever it is that horses eat."

"Hey, you'll love it."

"How do you know I'll love it? Have you ever eaten hay?"

"I mean you'll love riding Brownie."

And to Justin's great surprise, he did enjoy it. The little horse ambled along in an absentminded way, apparently occupied with his own thoughts. The two riders clip-clopped around the edge of the pasture, and even broke into a careful trot from time to time.

It took awhile, but Justin finally got to the place where he wasn't too nervous to ride and talk at the same time. "Isaiah seems like a nice guy," he said.

"Yeah, he is."

"Then how come you told me to hide my CD player when he showed up at the tent?"

Monique shrugged. "It's just a feeling I have. He's nice, but I think he's pretty desperate for Kenya shillings. Or better yet, U.S. dollars." She glanced back toward the riding club buildings."Especially when he hangs around with *those* two guys."

"What two guys?" Justin turned his head to look. Bad move. Just at that instant Brownie stumbled, and Justin had to grab the saddle horn with both hands just to stay on.

Isaiah was standing near the little white office building talking with two male teenagers. As Justin watched, all three stared in his direction.

"Who are they?" he asked.

"I'm not sure," Monique replied. "They showed up the other time I came here, but Isaiah didn't introduce us. I think they're his cousins or something. They give me a strange feeling."

"Why?"

Monique shivered. "They walk funny."

"Walk funny?"

"Like people who've been in prison."

Justin snickered in disbelief. "How do people who've been in prison walk?"

"Carefully. Like they don't want to get anybody mad at them. Ask your dad. I'll bet he can come into any room and spot the ex-cons right away."

The two teens were still talking to Isaiah when Monique and Justin rode up to the barn. Isaiah introduced them as Kenton and Malcolm Muchiri, his cousins on his mother's side. Malcolm was wearing a bright-green straw hat.

"Welcome to Kenya," said Kenton, who seemed like the more talkative one. "Do you like horses?"

Monique nodded. Justin shrugged.

"Malcolm and I work over there." Kenton jerked his thumb in the direction of the new racetrack next door. His voice lowered a bit, and his eyes flicked left and right. "Now Justin, I wonder if I could interest you in something that could make you a little money."

Justin cleared his throat. "No, thank you."

Kenton's eyebrows lifted in surprise. "You will not even allow me to explain?"

"Thanks, but I'm not interested."

"Let me understand this. An American boy who is not interested in money?"

Justin said nothing.

"Miss Monique, then," Kenton said persuasively. "Since your friend seems—so young and so shy, maybe you would be willing to listen to a tremendous opportunity I have for you."

"Sorry," she said quickly. "Not interested."

"I happen to know," he whispered, "who will win the 10:30 race tomorrow morning at the track."

"Everyone knows that," Isaiah said scornfully. "Bounding Bertie."

"That's the 2:30 race. I'm talking about the 10:30 race. And you keep out of this, Isaiah."

Monique asked in a distrustful voice, "How do you know who's going to win?"

Isaiah grinned. "The races are fixed. At least some of them are."

"What does that mean?"

"It means that somebody figures out in advance who will win, and tells the jockeys to make it happen that way."

"Yes," Kenton spoke again, "but I have inside information other people don't have about the 10:30 race, and if you let me invest some money for you, I can triple it."

"Sorry," said Monique.

"But," said Malcolm, speaking for the first time, "if you want a *really* good thing in which to put your money, try camels."

Justin happened to be watching Isaiah at that point, and saw him give a level glance at both his cousins, along with a side-to-side shake of his head.

"Well, sorry to trouble you," Kenton said quickly.

"Don't want to be a bother," Malcolm chimed in. "We really should be going. Come over and watch a race sometime. Let us know when you are coming. We can give you some very helpful tips."

"Very helpful," Kenton repeated. Malcolm gallantly lifted his green straw hat, then replaced it, and the two cousins turned their backs and sauntered off toward the racetrack.

"Sorry if my cousins were a bit pushy," Isaiah said. "They're a bit desperate for cash at the moment. They live in the shantytown, you know."

Justin blinked. "They do?"

"I thought," Monique said, "that they lived with you, since you're their relatives."

Isaiah looked at the ground, ashamed. "My father will not allow it."

"Why not?"

"Of course it's not really any of our business," Justin added quickly.

Isaiah sighed. "Kenton and Malcolm want to get very rich very fast. Father doesn't approve of some of their methods. I don't always agree with Father. By the way," he said anxiously, "please don't tell him they came here, will you?"

Justin suddenly felt a bit chilly in the African heat.

* * *

After Isaiah's shift was over, Mr. Kwendo drove them back to the shantytown. When he found out that Justin's dad hadn't yet rented a car, he insisted on driving the Cases downtown to their hotel.

"But first," he said to Dad as the two men and their sons left the shantys behind, "I want to show you something."

"What is it?" Isaiah wanted to know.

Mr. Kwendo glanced around at his son, who was sitting with Justin in the back seat. He stared steadily at him for a second, then looked back at the road. "Robert, I didn't tell you about this, because I want you to experience it like the boys will. You have never seen anything like this before, and I hope you never will again."

Chapter 3
Burning With Anger

Isaiah's father drove on in grim silence. Twenty minutes later they rounded a curve, and once they were beyond a grove of trees they saw a small column of light-gray smoke in a field. They drove toward it. Scores of cars—many of them police vehicles—were parked nearby, and a couple of hundred people stood around the flames. Mr. Kwendo parked his jeep, and the four of them joined the crowd.

"What's burning, *baba?"* Isaiah asked.

"Look," Mr. Kwendo said in a deep, harsh voice.

Justin stared at the fire. At first he thought he was looking at a huge pile of driftwood pieces, like he might find on an ocean shore. But then his stomach lurched.

"Dad," he whispered. "Those are *elephant tusks!"*

"That," said Mr. Kwendo angrily, "is indeed what they are."

Isaiah said, "But why are they burning them?"

"These tusks were confiscated from poachers. There are about six tons' worth here. Several years ago I watched as 27 tons were burned."

"But they're valuable!" Justin said.

"They are illegal," the ranger replied, "and no one should profit by them."

Robert Case had turned pale. "This is making me sick," he said. "Just think of all those elephants lying dead out there in the parks. And all for the tusks. This is horrible."

Mr. Kwendo nodded. "Now you see what we face here in Kenya." He stared at Dad. "You said it makes you sick. I am even more sick than you."

Dad nodded. "I can imagine it's doubly hard," he said gently, "for someone like you who sees these animals all the time."

Mr. Kwendo shook his head. "That is not what I mean." He reached out a muscular hand, placed it on Isaiah's shoulder and squeezed, hard. His son yelped with the pain, but the man did not release his grip. Instead, he drew the boy around to face him.

"Baba! Hapana!" Isaiah said in a trembly voice.

"Tell me the truth, and say it in English," Mr. Kwendo said. "When did you see Kenton and Malcolm last?"

Isaiah's eyes darted pleadingly to Justin's.

"When?"

"I saw them—"

"When?" his father roared.

"Today."

"Where?"

Isaiah's voice quivered. "At the riding club."

"What did they want?"

"Nothing."

"What," roared Mr. Kwendo, *"did they want?"*

"They wanted—money from me. And from J-Justin and Monique."

"Why?"

"I do not know."

Mr. Kwendo suddenly loosened his grip, and turned to Justin's dad. "Please tell me, Robert. What am I to do?"

Dad took a careful breath, but before he could speak the other man continued.

"My wife is auntie to those two boys. She cries to think of them living in the shantytown. Yet I will not have them in our house. They are a disgrace. They do not work at decent places. They should be back in Mombasa with their father, going to school, or learning real labor."

His body suddenly shuddered from head to foot. "But the real reason I do not want them in my house is that I do not want to know too much. I am afraid of what I might learn about them. I am charged with certain responsibilities. If I know something, I must report it. So I do not want to know."

Dad said in a low voice, "Do you think they're involved in . . . this?" He gestured toward the burning tusks.

"Oh, I do not think so. But the way they live might easily lead them to poaching. And then they are dead men. Walking dead men." Mr. Kwendo abruptly turned away. "I will take you to your hotel."

* * *

Later that evening Justin stood on the balcony outside the window of their tall hotel, CD player earbuds in place, watching the sunset slant over the Nairobi skyscrapers.

Soft music with a bit of a beat sounded in his ears:

Let me take you from this place,
Far away from steel and steam,
Far away from smoky towers,
To My soft, green fields of grace.

Shannon Fagin's delicate, childlike voice sounded as though she were singing for Justin alone. He'd read an article in a Christian youth magazine (which he'd also brought with him) which said Shannon was 15. Justin wished she was his sister, and that she had come along with him on this trip. Shannon would understand how he felt, even if Dad couldn't.

Of course, if she were his sister she probably wouldn't have her charming Irish accent, but speak the same boring way he did. OK, maybe she could be his friend, not his sister. Then she could teach him to sing "Green Fields of Grace."

He began to sing along with her.

Let Me free you from your fears,
Come away from dark and danger,
Come away from—

The CD player hiccupped, and Justin gave his belt pack a quick slap. But this time Shannon stopped singing for good. Snarling softly, Justin opened the battery compartment and switched the four AA batteries to new positions. But still Shannon refused to sing.

He stepped back through the sliding glass door into the brightly lit hotel room. He could hear his father speaking loudly and slowly to someone on the phone.

"—large aluminum packing case," Dad was saying. "No, about the size of an army footlocker. No, *foot locker,* not food locker. It will have my name on it—Robert Case. No, C-A-S-E. Have you seen it today? You haven't? Are you sure? Can you have someone check the baggage pickup areas in the whole airport? Well, please call me the moment it comes in. Thank you."

Not a good time to ask for batteries, Justin decided. He took the CD player out of his belt pack and put it in a drawer.

Dad hung up the phone and glanced at his son. "Hungry?"

"Yeah."

"Feel like Chinese?"

Justin blinked. "Chinese food? In Kenya?"

Dad grinned. "We'd better stick with what we know, for now. Jerry'll tip us off about good local Kenyan places later on. There's a Chinese restaurant just around the corner." He glanced toward the window. "Night isn't a good time to go wandering too far in Nairobi."

"Chinese is fine."

"Great." Dad walked over to a table and picked up something that looked like a bigger-than-average black walkie-talkie loaded with buttons and a telephone keypad. "Got room in that belt pack of yours for this?"

"What is it?"

"Didn't I show it to you?" Dad punched a few buttons on it, and there was a crackling and hissing. "This is the very latest in hand-held ham radio technology. An FM transceiver. Feel how heavy it is."

Justin took it in his hand. "Wow."

"Lots of circuitry inside there." Dad glanced around him. "I think the room here is pretty secure," he continued, "but this radio is something special. It cost Orville Frazier a lot of money, and I want to make sure I get it back to him. So would you mind slipping it into your pack there?"

"Sure," Justin said, doing it. *The reason there's room,* he thought bitterly, *is because my CD player's useless. Thanks to you, Dad.* "What does it take?" he asked, a bit too casually. "Double-A's?"

Dad shot a sharp glance at him. "Yes—nickel metal, hydride-rechargeable. But don't get any ideas. Hear?"

"OK," his son said hastily.

"We may not ever need that radio. But then again, we might."

"OK."

Five minutes later, Dad paused outside the red-and-gold door of the Seven Happiness Chinese restaurant. He pointed to several copies of a bright-orange poster, all taped to the restaurant windows.

"Camel racing," he muttered. "What will they think of next?"

Once inside, they settled into a booth with plush red cushions and place mats that offered Chinese wisdom. As Justin looked around, he thought, *This looks so familiar that we could almost be back home—except that almost everybody has dark skin, and they're probably talking Swahili.*

On the table was another of the orange posters.

"'Ship of the Desert Camel Racing, Limited,'" Dad read aloud. "'Fun for the whole family. New in Nairobi! Limited time only! Experience the adventure of racing a mile on camelback. Totally safe! Trained camel handlers present.'" He nudged his son under the table with his foot. "Want to sign up?"

Justin squinted in pain. "No way."

"What's the matter? Do you hurt somewhere?"

"I think I stretched some muscles I didn't know I had."

"On that horse this afternoon?"

"Yeah."

Dad studied the brochure some more, and sighed. "Well, this camel thing would be fun. Great photo opportunity too. But I guess we can't spare the time."

They ordered, and while they waited they talked about home and Mom and Justin's brother Robbie, who would be a college freshman that fall. They talked about Rico, and wondered how his Uncle Mike was doing in Belize. Then they talked about the safari, which would be starting in two days. And Dad's face wrinkled in a worried frown as he talked about the valuable aluminum foot locker the Walters were waiting for.

"It's got everything Jerry and Lucinda didn't bring along to start a little medical clinic," he said. "Orville Frazier talked to doctors and others who'd served overseas, and asked them what tools and medicines they needed most. And whatever they said to get, he went out and bought, then packed it in the footlocker. Aha," he said, "here comes chow."

The waiter arrived with a large round, black tray in one hand and a folding stand in the other, just like back home. Unfolding the stand with one hand, he placed the tray on it and began to unload dish after steaming dish.

"Want chopsticks?" Dad asked.

Justin, who had been staring hungrily at the food, looked at his dad as if the man had lost his mind. "No way."

Dad chuckled. "Just thought I'd check. Forks, please," he told the waiter, and the man smiled and hurried off.

"Do you like chow mein, Dad?"

Dad blinked. "Sure. Want some?"

"Then does that make you a chow mein-iac?" his son asked solemnly.

Dad rolled his eyes. "You're lucky you didn't crack one of those jokes at customs," he groaned. "They would have tried to confiscate them. But since they're so much a part of you, they would have had to keep you locked up too."

He leaned forward, and got serious. "What worries me about Frazier's medical box," he said in a low voice, "is this. It's one thing to pack valuable supplies in a wooden crate. I wish he had. But anyone who takes a look at that shiny metal case is going to say to himself, 'Whatever's inside there is worth big money.' And they'd be right."

"Uh, Dad. Can we eat?"

"Oh, sorry." They bowed their heads, and Dad thanked God for their food.

"But," Justin said after taking his first bite, "won't the box be safe at the airport when it gets here?"

Dad speared a piece of broccoli with his fork. "You

never know. Things are unpredictable in this part of the world. And people are so dreadfully desperate for money."

Justin nodded. "Like Isaiah. He wanted to trade me his thumb piano for my CD player."

"Oh?"

"I think he was serious. And his cousins tried to borrow some cash from me to bet it on a horse race."

"Don't you give them a single cent," Dad warned. "You'd never see your money—or them—again. You didn't, did you?"

"No way."

Dad shuddered. He put down his fork, reached out to get hold of Justin's wrist, and squeezed it gently. "I don't want you ending up as somebody's hostage, pal. Understand?"

"Yeah."

"Your mom would die if that happened."

Justin nodded.

"Kenya's loaded with bandits," Dad continued, "who just might take a kid hostage, a kid who looked rich, if they thought they could pull it off."

"I don't look rich."

"Oh yes you do, compared to them." Dad let go of Justin's arm. "Kendall and Malcolm might be OK, but Joseph Kwendo has his doubts about them. And even if they *are* fairly harmless, I'll bet you anything that they've got some dangerous friends. Everybody wants 'mon-nee.' "

After supper, when they entered the crowded hotel lobby, the man behind the desk raised his hand alertly.

"Mr. Robert Case?"

"That's me."

"I have a message for you." The man turned to a row of little boxes on the wall behind him, and came up with a slip of paper. "It was phoned in half an hour ago."

"Thanks," Dad said. Glancing at it, he put it in his pocket.

"Who's it from?" Justin asked.

"Let me tell you rule number one for travel in foreign lands where people are desperate for money," Dad said in a low voice as they crossed the lobby. "Don't mention names in hotel lobbies. A lot of people are hanging around here, probably hoping some juicy bit of news will turn up."

Back in the room, he took out the paper and looked at it again. Then he handed it to Justin.

"Sorry I missed you," it read. "Will call you again at 9:00. Jerry Walters."

At 9:05 the phone rang. Dad picked it up, said a few "oh's" and "yes's" and "you're kidding's" and "sounds like a plan's," and replaced the receiver.

"Guess what," he said. "You and I are going camel racing after all."

Wild Ride

"Camel racing?" Justin yelped. "Dad, I'm sore!"

Dad chuckled. "You'll feel better tomorrow."

"But I thought you said you couldn't spare the time."

"Dr. Walters really wants us to come," his father said. "Tomorrow is the Ship of the Desert Camel Company's first racing session, and they want publicity. So they've given out a lot of free tickets to journalists and TV stations. Someone told them about the Walters and the volunteer medical work they're doing in the shantytown, so the camel people got them some tickets too. Monique's giving some to the Kwendos."

"So Isaiah's coming too?"

"Yep."

"Well, OK," Justin said, wriggling doubtfully. "I guess I can always sit out the race instead of riding."

* * *

"Wow," Monique said in awe the next morning. "Look at all the people. Even this early."

Along with hundreds of people, they were standing in the sunshine next to a dirt road. A few men were pounding metal fence posts and stringing ropes to keep people away from the starting line.

"Where are the camels?" Justin asked.

Isaiah, his red thumb piano clamped between his palms, was thumbing out a bouncy little tune that made Justin's feet twitch. "They are probably still in the trucks," he said. "Or maybe at a watering tank." He held out the little instrument toward Justin as he played. "I bet you cannot do this with your CD player."

Justin grinned. "I can't do *anything* with my CD player."

"No?"

"I need more double-A's."

"Double-A's?"

"My batteries are dead."

Isaiah shrugged. "Get new ones."

Justin sighed. "Dad won't let me. He says I should forget the CD player and enjoy Africa. But there's this song I really like."

Monique said in a sultry voice, "Actually he's in love with Shannon Fagin."

"No, I'm not," Justin snapped.

Monique changed the subject. "Have you ever ridden a camel?" she asked Isaiah.

Isaiah suddenly stopped the music and handed the box to Justin. "You try. No, I have never ridden a camel," he said to Monique. "This is the first time the camel derby has come to Nairobi. Every year they have it in Maralal, about 200 miles north of here. But then some men formed the Ship of the Desert Company. Father said that they want to make camel racing a tourist attraction near the big cities such as Nairobi and Mombasa."

Justin flicked his thumbs at the stiff, flat metal pieces. The soft-sounding notes jangled together, out of tune. "How do you play this?" he asked.

"It is very easy," Isaiah said. "Do you see the longest one? Pluck it. Good. That is where the scale starts. Now strike the one to the left. Now the one to the right. Now the next one to the left. Left, right, all the way to each end. *Good.*"

After feeling around on the thumb piano for a minute or two, Justin was able to plunk out a jerky "Jesus Loves Me." Isaiah slapped him on the back approvingly.

A roar from the crowd made them glance up. A line of a dozen camels, each tugged along by a camel handler, was loping toward the crowd. The people parted quickly to let them through.

"Oh, they are so beautiful," Monique breathed.

Isaiah giggled. "Beautiful? *Lions* are beautiful. Camels are ugly."

"But I like the way their necks sort of curve," she explained. "And their faces look so . . . stately. Papa," she said, as Dr. Walters hurried up, "don't you think camels look stately?"

"Stately?" he repeated vaguely. "Here are your tickets, kids. Hang on to them. Put them in a pocket for now. One ticket will let you ride a camel for one race." He glanced around with a slightly worried look at the animals. "And that's all you'll probably want to ride. Be careful now. If you fall off, tuck and roll."

He glanced at Mr. and Mrs. Kwendo, who stood a few feet away talking with Justin's dad. "Joe? Helen? Robert? Want to ride?"

"Thank you, no," Mrs. Kwendo replied with a smile. The others declined as well, and Dr. Walters hurried off.

"I'm actually on duty," Joseph Kwendo said in his deep voice.

"On duty?" Dad said. "How come?"

"I was asked to make sure these animals were being treated well." He lowered his voice. "Also, I'm keeping my eye on some very unpleasant people."

Dad's glance flicked at the crowd. "Unpleasant people?"

Mr. Kwendo nodded. "I've just received word that there's a giant herd of elephants in Masai Mara Game Reserve."

Dad looked alert. "And you're wondering if poachers will try to get to them."

"That is correct. Anytime large herds gather, large numbers of poachers gather too. And since poachers are often involved with other moneymaking schemes"—the ranger gestured toward the crowd—"such as private gambling, I may see some familiar faces."

"I'm thirsty," Dad said suddenly. "Could you folks tip me off about the best—and safest—Kenyan soft drinks?"

The Kwendos both smiled. "Certainly," said Mrs. Kwendo, and the three of them headed for the refreshment stand.

Monique, Justin, and Isaiah quickly got in the racers' line, but were too far back for the first race. "That's good, though," Monique said thoughtfully. "This way we can learn what to do and what not to do from what happens to the first group."

Just as the first race began, two teenage boys hurried up to them. Isaiah saw them first and looked fearfully around.

"Kenton! Malcolm!" he hissed. Then he said something rapidly in Swahili. Justin heard the word *baba*.

"I know," Kenton replied in English, glancing nervously toward the refreshment stand. "Your father has eyes like an eagle, but he hasn't spotted us. We will be gone in a second." He looked pleadingly at Justin and Monique, and opened a little notebook. "I just wanted to give you two a chance to invest in the next camel race."

"You mean you want us to bet?" Monique asked.

"Certainly," he said. "I have inside information about which camel is fastest. Most of them go very slowly, but Simba is a strong racer. Nobody here knows this except the owners and handlers. So if you will each give me ten dollars, I can return a hundred to you in an hour. I promise."

"Sorry," Justin said automatically, remembering what Dad had told him.

"I'm afraid not," Monique said.

Kenton licked his lips nervously. "You are missing a good thing." He stared at them pleadingly for a moment more, then turned to Isaiah and asked, "Any shillings in your pockets?"

Isaiah sighed and switched to speaking Swahili again, using both his hands to gesture while his thumb piano bobbled on the end of its leather thong. Monique and Justin tactfully turned their attention to the race.

The race was an out-and-back one, which meant that the starting line was also the finish line. The idea was to ride like mad to the end of the line and then return, trying to dodge the slower camels coming at you. A few minutes later Justin saw the first camel returning. The crowd cheered wildly as the animal came loping closer and crossed the finish line.

"First place," said someone into a loud bullhorn, "goes to Simba and his rider!"

Monique and Justin stared at each other. "Kenton *did* know," she whispered. They both glanced around, expecting to hear the "I told you so's" of Kenton and Malcolm. But Isaiah and his cousins had vanished.

Finally all the camels had shuffled up to the finish line with their riders.

"Next team!" shouted the man into the bullhorn, and two smiling camel handlers beckoned to Justin and Monique.

"Where's Isaiah?" Monique asked, glancing around anxiously.

"I guess he'll have to wait for the next round," Justin replied.

The first youngster in line had claimed Simba, so Monique and Justin had to be content with other camels. Justin approached his camel cautiously.

"Do not be afraid," his handler said cheerfully, looping a large white cloth number over Justin's neck so that it hung down in front. "Her name is Nellie."

Nellie was sitting on the ground, her legs folded under her, and she stared at Justin for a moment in a bored way.

Strapped to her back was a crude saddle made of a rolled piece of foam rubber with what appeared to be a piece of leather on top. Stirrups hung down from either side, which the handler adjusted for Justin's legs.

"Justin!" Monique called to him. He glanced in her direction and saw that her camel had already stood up. "Wow. It's *high* up here!"

The handler shouted at Nellie several times, using some threatening Swahili comments it was probably better that Justin didn't understand. And suddenly Nellie's back legs unfolded, tipping Justin sharply forward. Desperately he grabbed the rear of the saddle, while several spectators laughed heartily. Then the camel unfolded her front legs too, and Justin found himself eight feet off the ground.

"Here, take these!" the handler called out. He put two ropes in Justin's hands, which connected to a sort of harness on Nellie's head. "Pull right if you want to go right, and left if you want to go left."

"Like a horse," Monique called from the top of her camel.

"But Nellie will go straight," the handler assured him. "She is a good camel. And here is a stick."

Justin found himself holding a wooden rod about as long as a yardstick. "What's this for?"

The handler grinned. "Hit her. Make her go."

The bullhorn blared, "Riders, get in line!"

Grabbing Nellie's head harness, the handler tugged. Nellie gave a loud bray that sounded like a donkey speaking into a bullhorn. As she lollopped forward toward a long yellow rope held chest-high by two men, Justin dug his heels firmly into her side and discovered just how sore his horseriding muscles were.

"Hang on, Justin!" Monique shouted with a delighted grin.

"Five," blared the bullhorn. "Four . . . three . . . two . . ."

The noise of the crowd drowned out the last of the count. As the yellow rope dropped, most of the camels surged forward. But not Nellie. Instead, she turned her head and glared at Justin, then promptly headed in the opposite direction! Her handler, who seemed to be expecting this, leaped for her harness and howled Swahili into her ear. The camel seemed to snarl at the handler, and finally headed off in the direction the other racers had gone.

Swaying high atop her back, Justin was horrified. He had been expecting the ride to be something like being on a horse, only faster. Instead, Nellie galloped in a swaying, stomach-lurching, side-to-side way. Justin's leg muscles were growing more sore, but he didn't dare relax. And he didn't dare slow down either, because he didn't want to dodge all the camels that would soon be coming back toward him.

A few seconds later, Nellie lost interest in the race again, and slowed so abruptly that Justin almost fell off the front of the saddle.

"Nellie, come on!" he pleaded.

She paid no attention.

Justin raised his voice a little. "Nellie?"

There was a shuffling sound up ahead. A camel was returning, with a boy seated high atop the animal. "Use the stick!" he called. "Yell at her."

So Justin shouted at Nellie and smacked her sharply on the rump. She snarled, but began to shuffle a little faster, and when they finally made it to the half-mile mark, another handler grabbed her halter, turned her around, and headed her back.

As soon as Nellie ambled across the finish line, she promptly folded herself up, and Justin crawled off her back. His legs were not only sore, but they felt like rubber, and his stomach was queasy. Justin staggered uncertainly toward Monique.

"What's wrong?" she asked him.

"Aren't you sore?"

"Not really," she said. "Of course, it's different than riding a horse."

"Lots different," Justin moaned. "On a horse you're not eight feet up in the sky. And you don't get seasick."

"Do you know why you got seasick?"

Justin frowned. "Because she was swaying so much, that's why."

"No, I mean, do you know *why* she was swaying so much?"

Justin shook his head, and suddenly wished he hadn't.

"While I was riding," she said, "I was watching the other camels, and I noticed the way they walk. A horse moves its legs in a way that makes the ride smooth. But when a camel trots, both its left legs go forward while both its right legs go back. That makes it bounce and sway more."

"Monique." With the back of his hand, Justin wiped the sweat off his forehead.

"What?"

"Can we talk about something else besides bouncing and swaying?"

"Sure. Let's go find Isaiah."

"OK."

As the two of them threaded their way through the crowd, Justin thought about how cheerful everyone seemed. He remembered Dad talking about how poor the country was, and how much unemployment there was, but these people were smiling and happy. And Justin remembered how his dad had told him that money can't buy happiness.

A half hour later they happened to pass Justin's dad and Monique's mom, who were chatting.

"Justin," Dad said, "don't wander too far. We're going to go over and help the Walters pack up their things and get it into storage. Be back here in 15 minutes."

"OK," Justin responded, looking at his watch. As they moved off, he glanced at Monique. "You're packing up the clinic? How come?"

She shrugged. "No more supplies. We're totally out of baby kits, and there's not much else either. We were counting on Mr. Frazier's box to get here by now." She sighed. "But maybe it's all for the best. Mom and Dad really need a break. They're looking forward to this safari at least as much as I am."

"How are they going to get the Land Rover on the train?"

"They're not," she said. "I'm going with you and your dad on the train, and they'll drive the Land Rover."

"Cool. Whoa—there goes another race," Justin said, as wild cheering erupted again from the crowd. "I wonder who's got Nellie now?"

"Look," Monique said quickly. "Here comes Mr. Kwendo. Maybe he knows where Isaiah is."

Joseph Kwendo was striding quickly toward them, his lips firm. "Good morning again," he said. "Did you have a good camel ride?" Without waiting for their answer, he said, "My son Isaiah. Do you know where he is?"

Monique shook her head. "No, we've been looking for him ever since the camel races started."

Mr. Kwendo stared around him uneasily. "Nobody has seen him since we arrived this morning," he said. "I hope nothing has happened to him."

CHAPTER 5

The Green Hat

Mr. Kwendo strode away.

"What do you think happened to him?" Monique asked her friend. "Do you think they kidnapped him?"

"I doubt it." Justin scanned the crowd again. "They don't seem like guys who'd do something like that."

"They seemed really jumpy."

"Yeah, almost desperate. But kidnapping? I don't think so."

But Isaiah was still missing late that afternoon when Helen Kwendo suddenly appeared at the Walters' silver Land Rover in the shantytown. Dad and Dr. Walters had gone to visit one of the clinic patients. Monique, her mother, and Justin had just finished packing the clinic tent and all its contents into a large trailer, which Jerry Walters planned to park in a secure storage unit.

"Helen!" Surprise sounded in Lucinda Walters' voice. "Are you all right?"

Mrs. Kwendo's polite smile trembled. "Yes. I mean . . ." her voice trailed off.

"However did you get all the way out here? I thought you didn't drive."

"I . . . took a bus."

"A bus? All the way across town?" Mrs. Walters stared at the distant Nairobi skyscrapers. "You must have had to walk too."

"Yes. A long way."

"Well, you're sure not walking back. Jerry will take you home. But what's wrong?" Mrs. Walters glanced at Monique and Justin, then back to the other woman. "Shall I send the kids away?"

Mrs. Kwendo shook her head. "I—" she began, but found she couldn't speak. She fumbled in a red-and-black woven bag she carried. "I have something for—" She glanced up. "Your name is Jason?"

"Justin," the boy corrected.

She drew out a red wooden box, about the size of a fat paperback book.

"Isaiah's thumb piano!" Monique gasped.

Justin's face went numb. "Is Isaiah . . . OK?"

"Yes. He is fine." Mrs. Kwendo held out the little box. "He told me that he wanted you to"—and her voice broke—"keep it s-safe for him."

Mrs. Walters put her arm around the sobbing woman and led her to the open passenger door of the Land Rover. "Sit down there," she said gently. "And you can tell us just as much, or just as little, as you want to. But we're here to help however we can."

The others gathered around her, and after a few trembly breaths, Mrs. Kwendo grew calmer. "My husband does not know I am here," she said. "Please do not tell him."

"We certainly won't," Mrs. Walters assured her. "But

Isaiah is safe, you say?"

"Isaiah is in Mombasa," said the other woman.

"Mombasa?"

"That is, he *will be* in Mombasa in a few hours."

Monique asked, "With Kenton and Malcolm?"

Justin cleared his throat. "We saw them with Isaiah this morning."

Mrs. Kwendo nodded. "I saw them, but my husband did not. They were trying to hide from him. But they found me alone, and we talked." She sighed a heavy sigh. "Their father—my brother—lives in Mombasa. I told Kenton and Malcolm it is time for them to go back and find good work with people they know. I have told them to leave the shantytown—it is no place for them. Then they ask Joseph, and Joseph too says, leave. But they don't obey."

"Did you finally convince them to go back home?" Mrs. Walters asked sympathetically.

"On one condition."

"That Isaiah go along?" Monique guessed.

"Yes. But just for a little while. He has visited his cousins several times there. They are good boys," Mrs. Kwendo insisted. "And my brother is a good man. But Kenton and Malcolm believe that they can become rich very quickly. My brother wants to help them learn that good wealth comes slowly."

"How are they traveling?" Mrs. Walters asked anxiously.

"By train."

"We're leaving by train tomorrow," Monique said. "But we're going in the opposite direction."

Mrs. Kwendo sighed. "And I suppose I will have to tell Joseph the whole story tonight. He will not like it. But I think he will see that it is the best way to get everyone safely away from trouble. After all, he will be gone a lot in the next few weeks, because he needs to help protect the elephant herd."

Mrs. Walters said, "Well, we'll be praying that everything goes well."

"Oh," Mrs. Kwendo said, "I almost forgot. Justin, Isaiah told me to tell you something. He made me repeat it to him so I got it right. He said, 'Tell Justin that a thumb piano doesn't need double-A batteries.'"

Justin grinned. He put the leather thong around his neck. Holding the edges of the box between his palms, he plucked a few notes. "I'll keep this safe," he said, "until I see him again."

It was actually Dad and Justin who drove Mrs. Kwendo to her home. She told Mr. Case the whole story on the way. When the group pulled up beside the little house, Mrs. Kwendo thanked Justin's dad many times, and even offered to pay for the ride. Dad rejected the suggestion firmly.

"God bless," he said. "We'll be praying for you."

As they drove away, Justin glanced back and shuddered. "Did you see the jeep, Dad? Mr. Kwendo's home."

Dad nodded. "Uh-huh. It's going to be fairly tense around the Kwendo supper table tonight. But maybe it's all for the best. The bottom line is this: Mombasa is east—way out east on the coast—and the Masai Mara game park is west. Lots and lots of beautiful African landscape in between. That should make Joseph feel better."

Back at the hotel, they began to pack.

"Let's get everything ready to go before we head to bed," Dad said.

"I thought the train doesn't leave until tomorrow night."

"True, but I've got a lot of places to go tomorrow. Let's just check out first thing in the morning and take our luggage with us."

Justin fingered a small black box with a cord attached. "What's this?" he asked.

"Battery charger for the FM transceiver. "

"Oh, yeah, that ham radio thing," Justin said thoughtfully.

Dad was a quick packer, and an even quicker getter-to-sleeper. Soon muffled snores began to sound from his bed. Justin, however, found himself wide awake, in a mood that was getting gloomier all the time.

I miss Mom, he thought to himself. *I miss Rico. I miss Robbie, although I don't miss his tickling me whenever he feels like it. But I do miss playing catch with him.*

He reached over to the bedstand and picked up the thumb piano. *Now's a good time to figure this thing out,* he thought. *Maybe if I learn it in the dark, I'll do better on it.* He plunked a few notes softly, and tried to do the scale. But then he got to thinking about Isaiah, and his laugh, and the tense, fearful Swahili he had used as he talked to Kenton and Malcolm.

Maybe I'll never see Isaiah again. A tear trickled out of the corner of Justin's left eye and started to run down his cheekbone. He sniffed. *And I probably won't get to keep this thumb piano, because his mom will want it.*

Justin buried his head in his pillow and began crying softly.

After a while he slithered sideways out of the bed and tiptoed to the dresser where the FM transceiver lay. Carrying it over to the window, he found the crack between the curtains, and in the dim light from the neon signs he studied the unit carefully.

Aha, here's where the batteries go, he thought. Sure enough, he pressed his thumb and pulled and the lid came off. And there he found a beautiful nest of four double-A nickel metal, hydride-rechargeable batteries. *Now that I know what the charger looks like, I can use these batteries and secretly recharge them anytime I want to.*

Soon he was back in bed listening to Shannon's adorable Irish voice on the CD player.

Let Me take you from this place,
Far away from steel and steam,
Far away from smoky towers,
To My soft, green fields of grace.

Let Me free you from your fears,
Come away from dark and danger,
Come away from guilt and shame,
Come and let me dry your tears
In My soft, green fields of grace.

And in the morning, when Dad was in the shower,

Justin replaced the batteries in the transceiver.

* * *

"Why do they call it the Lunatic Line?" Justin asked.

It was almost 7:00 p.m. Justin and his dad stood on the platform of the Nairobi railway station waiting for the Walters to arrive with Monique. Through the night, the train would take them westward to Nakuru, a little over halfway to Lake Victoria. There they would get off, and Dad would find a bus south to the Masai Mara game reserve.

"Well, to answer your question," Dad said, "back in the late 1890s Kenya was called British East Africa. The British decided they needed a railroad across Kenya."

"What about the 'lunatic' thing?" Justin pressed.

Dad grinned. "At that time, there was nobody out there to ride it. Nobody who wanted to, that is. There were very few European settlers, and the local tribespeople simply didn't travel by train. Still the British built the railroad. Took 'em three years."

"But the British were right, weren't they?"

Dad glanced uneasily at his watch. "Well, yes and no. Sometimes the track going west washes out. And it takes a whole lot longer than Jerry and Lucinda's Land Rover is going to take them."

"So Monique wants to ride with us?"

"That's what she says. Aha. There they are. Jerry," he shouted, "what held you up?"

"Sorry," the man said, staggering toward them with a

suitcase. “If you had a daughter, you’d understand, Robert. She’s got enough things in this suitcase to start her own clothing boutique.”

Monique, who was following him with her mother, snorted. “Dad, that’s not true and you know it.” She seized the handle and took the suitcase from him. “You guys have a good trip,” she told her parents. Hugs and kisses were exchanged.

“We’ll join you in a couple of days,” her father said. “If the Land Rover doesn’t break down, of course. You pray for us, and we’ll pray for you.”

“Will do,” Dad replied. “OK, kids,” he said after they’d waved goodbye until the Land Rover had disappeared around a corner. “Listen very carefully. I got us two first-class compartments right next to each other. Monique, you’ll have yours all to yourself, and Justin and I will take the one next to it.”

“Sounds great!” she said. “Thanks for taking me with you.”

“You deserve a break, nurse.”

Monique sighed. “I was going bananas in that shantytown. I just pity the people who have to live there all the time.”

Dad nodded. “But you and your folks made a real difference. That’s why Orville Frazier is sponsoring this safari for you. OK, look sharp.” A rustling along the platform told them that the train was about to depart. “Look down there. See those cars? That’s third class. If you kids want to explore the train, do it together. Always. But don’t go into third class."

"Why not?" Justin asked.

"Because Joseph Kwendo said not to. He says that's where some dangerous people travel."

"And the poor people too," Monique said as she watched a final few passengers getting aboard.

"If it was just the poor, that would be one thing," Dad said firmly. "So don't go down there. OK, let's hustle. Justin can carry that humongous suitcase of yours," he said to Monique with a chuckle.

"It's not heavy!" she said, holding on firmly to the handle.

As they walked down the narrow hallway next to their coach's outer windows, the train suddenly jerked and creaked beneath them. Justin felt a tingle of excitement. *We're off on another adventure,* he thought. *I wonder where it will lead us.*

As he and Dad settled into their cozy compartment, they could hear Monique squealing with delight beyond the connecting door. A couple of quick knocks sounded. "May I come in?" she called.

"Sure," Dad answered.

"This is incredible!" she said. "I don't know how I'm going to ever get to sleep tonight. Just think," she said, pointing to the window where Nairobi buildings were gliding past. "While we're sleeping, out there in the darkness there are going to be lions and elephants and giraffes."

Mr. Case chuckled. "I think the beasties are mainly in the game parks. But you never know. And don't forget the Cape buffalo."

"The Caped Buffalo?" asked his son. "Is that a superhero comic?"

"Cape buffalo," Dad growled. "Keep him in line, Monique. I can't."

Justin got to his feet. "You said we could explore, right?"

"Right. But—"

"—don't go into third class," Justin said. "Got it. Come on, Monique."

Monique locked her hallway compartment door, and the two of them strolled single file down the hall.

"What do you think of Africa so far?" she asked him.

"It's an exciting place," he said. "I just wish Isaiah could have come along on this trip."

"I see you're still wearing his thumb piano."

"Yeah." Justin thumbed a few moody notes.

"That crazy guy," Monique said. "What's so great about Mombasa that he had to go there? I mean, Isaiah's dad's got a great job. Think of all the free safaris Isaiah probably gets to go on."

"He wants 'mon-nee.'"

Monique sighed. "I guess if you've never had it, you want it pretty badly." As she came to the connecting door between the two cars, she paused. "How do we tell when we get to third class?"

"Just look for poor people, I guess."

In the second car Justin noticed that the compartments were bigger, and decided that it was second class because more people had to fit into one compartment. Four cars later he came to a stop.

"Third class," he said, pointing.

They stared out through the glass door window, across the open space between the two train cars, and in through the other window.

"No compartments there," Justin said. "Just seats, like a bus. Old seats. Some facing this way, and some facing the other way."

The third-class car was crowded. Some of the people were standing, and Justin could see wooden boxes piled on the floor.

"Look," Monique said, "someone's got a chicken on their lap. And there's a dog."

Justin suddenly pressed his elbow against hers.

"Ouch," she said.

"Look. On the right-hand aisle. Sitting facing the other direction."

She hiccupped. "The green hat?"

"Where have I seen that hat before?"

"Malcolm had a hat like that," she said thoughtfully. "But there are probably millions of green hats in Africa."

"That's Malcolm!" Justin said.

"You can't be sure," Monique responded. "And anyway, what's he doing here? He's in Mombasa with Kenton and Isaiah."

The green hat suddenly turned sideways, and they saw the wearer's face.

"Malcolm," they both whispered.

CHAPTER 6

On the Road

"What's he doing *here?"* Justin asked.

Monique moved sideways. "He's gonna see you if he looks around."

"I *want* him to see me," Justin said.

"How come?"

"I want to ask him how Isaiah's doing."

"Your dad said not to go into third class."

"But if he comes out, we can talk to him."

"Look," she said. "Look who he's talking to."

Justin stared through the window. "Hey. I recognize that guy."

"So do I."

Justin unzipped his belt pack, got out his scope, and clapped it to his eye. "That's the guy who was at the camel races."

"Let me look." She took the little half binocular and focused it. "You're right. He was sort of supervising the handlers. Good eye, Super Snoop."

"Don't call me Super Snoop."

"Why not?"

"It reminds me of the bad parts of the Red Mary mystery, before things got better." He focused the scope on

Malcolm's conversation partner again. "Oh-oh. The guy's mad."

"Mad at Malcolm?"

"Looks like it. There's his fist. No, maybe not. But he's got this scowly look on his face. Malcolm's nodding. Now he's shaking his head. Now he's—"

"Let's go," Monique said quickly. "Now. Duck and run, Justin!"

Malcolm had risen quickly to his feet and removed his hat. Justin and Monique turned their backs and scrambled down the hall for a while, until Justin turned and glanced behind him.

"Is he coming?" Monique gasped.

"No."

Slowing their pace, they walked casually back toward their own car. Just before they knocked at the Case compartment door, Monique dug her elbow into Justin's.

"Better tell your dad," she said.

"Yeah," Justin agreed.

"Well, well," Robert Case said after they'd told him what they'd seen. "If you're sure it was Malcolm, it does indeed make one wonder what he's doing here. You didn't see his brother? Or Isaiah?"

They shook their heads.

"I've got an idea." Dad stood up, bracing himself against the sway of the train, and picked up his camera from the top bunk. "Justin, you stay here and watch our things. Monique, let's you and I go see if we can spot the guy Malcolm was talking to, and I'll try to get his picture."

Monique asked, "But where will you get the film developed?"

"It's a digital camera," Justin said. "You can see the picture right away."

Dad nodded. "And it's got a pretty good zoom lens. So if we can spot him at all, it won't be a problem to get a close-up."

Twenty minutes later they were back.

"We had to do a lot of pretending to look out the window and admire the scenery," Dad said, "but finally he moved to where we could see him clearly. I got several shots through the door window. I'll dump them onto my laptop, and when I get to a phone jack I'll e-mail them back to Nairobi to see if this fellow is on a wanted list."

They went to the dining car, and Dad ordered supper from a white-gloved waiter. As they ate and talked together, the sky grew darker outside the window by their table. Justin stared into the darkening forests and thought about soft, green fields of grace.

Back in their compartments, Dad read two or three newspapers he'd picked up at the train station while Justin and Monique played chess with Dad's travel set. The gentle rocking and the steady clicking of the tracks made them sleepy, and when Dad suggested they turn in, he didn't have to beg. Justin was able to sneak the CD player and the transceiver into the top bunk, do the battery swap, and listen to Shannon again.

When the pale morning light woke him, he felt his CD player under his shoulder. His earbuds had come out.

But the disk was still spinning.

The shock made him instantly wide-awake. *The charger,* he thought. *I've got to get the batteries into the—but no. The charger's not gonna work on the train.*

His fingers fumbled stiffly with the CD, spilling the batteries onto the bedsheet. Thankfully the player hadn't crashed to the floor during the night, waking Dad. Justin slipped the batteries into the transceiver and carefully snapped the lid shut. And later, when Dad got up to go to the bathroom, he put it back in Dad's bag.

When the train squeaked to a halt in Nakuru, the three of them stepped out on the sunny platform.

"Goodbye, train," said Monique, looking back over her shoulder at it. "I'm sorta going to miss you." The three travelers peered around, but caught no glimpse of Malcolm or the camel handler.

Dad easily found a huge dusty silver bus bound for the game park. "Don't bother getting on just yet," he said.

"When's it leaving?" Justin asked.

"Nobody knows."

"Nobody *knows?*"

Dad nodded. "The driver won't leave until all the seats are full. We'll just wait until we see people starting to get on. So stick close."

"I don't believe this," Justin whispered to Monique two hours later. "What time is it?"

She glanced at her watch, then grinned. "Who needs a watch in Kenya? Things will happen when they happen."

The sun was hot, and they were still sitting in the

shade of the bus watching two boys who looked like third-graders crouching on either side of a thick slab of wood. The wood had been hollowed out into several shallow holes, and one after another the kids scooped up rocks from some of the holes and dropped them one by one into other holes.

Dad, who was reading a small paperback book, yawned. "What's that game they're playing?" he asked.

"Mancala, I think they call it," Monique answered. "The kids in the shantytown played it all the time."

A shout from the driver got everybody moving. Women in colorful robes hoisted large packages and shoved them through the bus door ahead of them. The bus rumbled, cleared its throat, and began to move.

As they rode through the countryside, Monique and Justin stared out the windows. The blue sky was huge, and the trees they saw were tough and scrubby.

"I thought Africa had jungles," Justin told her. "A lot of this looks like prairie."

"Africa's got all kinds of country," she said.

"Where are the elephants?"

Dad glanced around. "Farmers don't like them," he said. "So you won't see a lot of them until we get to the game parks. They travel in families."

"Farmers travel in families?"

Dad reached over and tried to tickle him. *"Elephants,* you rascal."

Monique rolled her eyes.

"Knock, knock."

"Nobody's home," Monique replied flatly.

"Come on," he said. "Knock, knock."

"Who's there?"

"Who."

"I know that one," she said. "I'm gonna say, 'Who, Who,' and you're gonna say, 'I didn't know you were an owl.' "

He snapped his fingers in disgust, then said, "OK then. Knock, knock."

"Who's there?"

"Ah."

"Ah who?"

"Sorry about your allergies."

She stared at him. "Allergies?"

"Ah who," Justin said. "It's sorta like ah-choo. You know, what you say when you sneeze. When you have allergies. Knock, knock."

"Justin," Dad said,"that's probably enough."

Monique suddenly asked, "When poachers kill elephants do they kill the babies too?"

Dad shrugged. "I'm not sure. The main goal is to get ivory, and lots of it, so maybe they let the babies go."

"But," Justin said, "if the parents are killed, the babies are orphans."

"You've got it. And there's nobody to protect them from the lions."

Late that evening they arrived at Keekoruk Lodge, just a few miles from the Tanzanian border, and checked into their suite of rooms.

"How's the phone service in Kenya?" Dad asked Monique.

"Pretty miserable," she said. "My dad sometimes has to spend hours trying to get through to someone. But maybe at night it's better."

"I'm going to try and call Joseph Kwendo and get an e-mail address for either the park service or the police."

After wrestling with Information for a while, Dad finally got the Kwendos' number. After another 15 minutes' work, his face suddenly brightened.

"Helen? This is Robert Case. How are you?" There was a pause, and Justin saw Dad's face grow tense. "Helen, you'll have to slow down. I didn't pick up the last part of what you . . . Helen . . . Helen? May I speak to your husband?"

There was a pause. Dad sat down in a chair by the desk.

"What's wrong?" Justin hissed.

Dad put his hand over the receiver. "I don't know," he whispered. "I'm not used to her accent, and she was crying, so I couldn't really—Joseph? Is that you? I couldn't understand what Helen was saying there at the last. Something about Isaiah being—" He broke off and listened.

Monique crouched down to where she was right in front of his eyes. "Isaiah being *what?*" she whispered.

Dad shook his head and closed his eyes so he could concentrate.

CHAPTER 7
Suspect in the Sky

"When, Joseph?" Dad said into the phone, eyes still shut. "When did they leave?" Suddenly his eyes popped open wide. "Wait a minute. If that's true, all three of those boys must have been on our train!"

Justin and Monique stared at each other.

"OK, look," said Dad. "Give me an e-mail address where I can send some digital photos." He began to tell Mr. Kwendo about the man Malcolm had been talking to.

"Why," Monique asked Justin softly, "would they be coming this direction? And how did they get back from Mombasa so fast?"

"Maybe they never went to Mombasa at all."

"I guess not." She glanced at Justin's dad, who was now copying down an e-mail address and reading it carefully back into the receiver.

"Take a look at these shots as quickly as you can," Dad said. "And get somebody to e-mail me back any data. We're going to do the balloon safari tomorrow—not the long one, just the day trip. We'll be back here tomorrow night."

He hung up the phone, and took a deep breath and let it slowly out.

"Our safari's on hold," he finally said. "Not the balloon

one; we do that tomorrow. But there's some pretty serious news."

"What happened?" Justin asked.

"Helen Kwendo called her brother in Mombasa to see if the guys had arrived there safely. And he hadn't seen them—hadn't even heard from them. So he and Helen decided to wait until this morning when the next train was due in, to see if they'd taken that one instead. They didn't show up."

"So they didn't take the Mombasa train," Monique said thoughtfully. "They took ours."

"Maybe so, maybe not," Justin said. "After all, the only one we saw was Malcolm."

"That's what worries me a little," Dad said. "Why weren't they all sitting together? Of course, Malcolm could have walked to that car from another car just to talk to the older man. You said you thought he was connected with the camel races."

Justin nodded. "He seemed like a boss or a supervisor or something."

"Well, it could all be very innocent." Dad got to his feet and yawned. "Not normal, and not healthy for the boys, but legal. Maybe the camel man is checking out new sites for camel racing, and hired the boys to come along and scotch-tape those orange posters to store windows. Monique."

"What?"

"When did your folks say they'd get here?"

"They had some things to do in Nairobi," she said, "so they planned to get here by tomorrow afternoon."

"So we'll touch base with them after the balloon ride. OK, young'uns," Dad said, "you'd better get some sleep. The desk clerk told me they launch the balloons pretty early."

Two seconds before drifting to sleep, Justin remembered that he hadn't listened to Shannon Fagin all day. There was something, however, that he didn't remember—to charge the transceiver's batteries after Dad went to sleep.

* * *

Dad got them up so early the next morning that Justin didn't actually remember getting dressed. "I'm starving," he mumbled.

"I've got breakfast for all of us in my backpack," Dad said. "Move, move. The balloon will go up without us."

"I'll stay down and watch you," his son said in a foggy voice.

"Hey, hey. You'll love it."

Monique wandered in from the bathroom, staggering slightly. "Justin hates flying," she said sleepily.

"Nonsense," Dad said briskly, clipping the radio transceiver to his belt and slipping his arms into a large backpack. "Ballooning isn't flying. Nothing like it. No wings, no engines. Easy up, easy down. A good long flight, then they settle down in the middle of nowhere and we have a sit-down meal at tables, right out in the open. Then a bus brings us back here."

Soon they were standing with several other people in the cool air just a few yards from a huge square wicker basket lying on its side. Justin noticed that the bottom was wood braced with additional planks. A hoarse, thunderous roar shattered the early morning calm, and woke him up all the way.

"What's that?" he yelped.

"The burners," Dad said. "They're heating the air inside the balloon."

Three men in orange overalls stood at the mouth of the balloon. One was holding a thin metal tube that came out of the end of a long hose. White flames with orange edges came out of the end of the pipe, and slowly the red, orange, yellow, blue, and green balloon panels began to fill out.

Monique stared upward as the giant balloon straightened above them. By then the basket had tipped upright, its braced bottom on the grass.

"All aboard!" shouted a man who was evidently the pilot. He climbed inside and reached above him, and a couple of quick roars sounded. The basket moved slightly on the grass, and the three men in orange overalls held the edges down.

"I don't want to go," Justin said in a small voice.

"Come on," Monique said briskly. She jumped up and balanced with her tummy on the rim of the basket. The pilot grinned and helped her over. Several other people clambered aboard, including Dad, before Justin got up his courage. Finally, with sweaty fingers, he gripped the rim of the basket and scrambled over. Isaiah's thumb piano clunked against the basket as he landed inside. Dad had managed to get a corner seat, and Monique and Justin sat on either side of him.

More deafening thunder from just over their heads, this time a long roar. The basket creaked and crackled, and began to rise above the heads of the men in overalls.

"This is so *cool!"* Monique gasped.

The ground fell away faster than Justin had expected it would. But everything was smooth and silent, except when the burner thundered above them.

"Got that scope of yours with you, Justin?" Dad asked.

His son slapped his belt pack and nodded.

"You're going to need it."

The pilot laughed. "Yes! We see many animals today!"

Parked securely in his corner, Dad zipped open his backpack and brought out fruit leather, a snack mix, energy bars, oranges, bananas, and a plastic sack to put the peels in. As Justin ate he felt the cool air and the solidness of the basket floor underfoot and decided that a balloon flight wasn't so bad after all.

"I understand," one of the other passengers said, "that there's a large herd of elephants somewhere near here." Justin glanced around just in time to see the pilot, with his grin still on his face, look suddenly upward and turn the burner on. But the pilot said nothing in response to the passenger's comment.

On they sailed through the sky. To Justin it seemed as if they were above a huge sandbox in which someone had placed toy animals—except that the animals were real.

"Down there!" Monique squealed. "In that river! What *are* those?"

Justin and several other passengers looked over the rim of the basket, straight down to where she was pointing. Six or eight black objects that looked like smooth, black peanuts floated in the water.

"Hippos," said the pilot. "They are staying cool."

Dad bent close to Justin's ear. "Look off to the left. And be quiet."

Justin glanced to his left, and saw nothing. "Where?" he whispered.

"Out close to the horizon. Get your scope. A bit to the left of that mountain range. You can just barely see them."

Justin fumbled for his scope and soon had it to his eye, sweeping and sectoring like his Dad had taught him. Suddenly he saw them, partly shadowed by a dark gray cloud.

"Dad. That's—"

Dad's hand came gently around his son's head and over his mouth. "And look down there," he said in a conversational tone, pointing in a different direction. "Those are giraffes, aren't they? No, I guess not."

But Justin didn't look down. He looked around him at the rest of the passengers, searching for something his father must have already seen. But everybody looked like ordinary, slightly sunburned tourists.

"I have a question for you," the pilot suddenly said, looking around at his passengers. "What is Kenya's most dangerous animal?"

"The lion," someone said.

"Sorry, that is not right."

"The elephant?" someone else suggested.

Monique poked Justin. "Help me out," she told him softly. "What animal did your dad say to watch out for? Something to do with a superhero."

"Cape buffalo," Justin said loudly.

The pilot's grin faded a bit, as though he had wanted to be the one to tell the answer. "That is right," he said. "Look down there, to my right. There are several together there, drinking from that stream. When they are in a herd they are not as dangerous. But one buffalo alone, or two together, often attack humans. Buffalo kill more people in Kenya than lions or elephants do. Study them carefully now, so you will know them if you meet them again."

But Justin noticed something interesting. As the passengers gazed obediently down at the buffalo herd, the pilot lifted a large pair of binoculars to his eyes. He was focusing them in the direction Dad had pointed out to Justin earlier—out to a vast elephant herd beneath a darkening cloud near the horizon.

Dad noticed what the pilot was doing. Grinning foolishly like an ordinary tourist, he lifted his camera and took a casual picture of the pilot. By the time the man had lowered the binoculars, Dad's camera was pointing earnestly down toward the buffalo herd.

Forcing himself to take his eyes off the pilot, Justin stared down at them, wondering what he could do to help

Dad. He wished he could whisper to Monique, but Dad had said not to.

Suddenly the pilot spoke a couple of words that sounded like Swahili. And at the same time, Dad put his arm around Justin and bent his head close to his son's ear again.

"Don't look, but he's got a two-way radio," Dad said. "See if you can get close to him to see what his frequency is. Memorize the numbers on the display. Learn them in groups of two, such as 23, 52, 96."

The pilot said something in Swahili again. He seemed to be trying to get someone's attention.

Justin stepped away from the rim and threaded his way around the passengers' feet to a spot just behind the pilot. A couple of people moved aside to make room for him on their part of the bench. Looking back, he saw that the pilot's shoulder just hid his number display. So taking his courage in his hands, Justin took hold of a rope, put his foot on the bench, and stood up.

Don't look down, he said to himself. *Look at the display. Memorize it in twos. One-four, three-five—*

"Hey, young man," said a passenger in a worried voice, "you'd better get down from there."

The pilot said the same Swahili phrase again. His radio squawked back at him.

One-four, three-five—

"Sir," the passenger said to Dad, "I don't think your boy had better be—"

"Son," Dad said with false cheerfulness, "get down from there."

One-four, three-five, zero.

And then Justin looked down beyond the basket's rim, and his fingers froze to the rope. *I'm going to fall,* he thought. *I'm going to let go and fall over the edge, down on top of that buffalo herd.*

The pilot turned, and scowled just as Justin glanced back at him.

One-four, three . . .

Justin forced a grin, released the rope, stepped down from the bench, and scrambled over beside Dad, who had now turned so that he was kneeling on the bench and was gazing out over the basket's corner. A voice came from the pilot's radio, and the pilot burst into earnest Swahili.

To Justin's horror, he saw that Dad held the transceiver in his hand, down inside the corner of the basket where nobody could see it. Somehow he'd also managed to bring his little digital voice recorder close to the radio's speaker. The red light on the recorder was on.

"The numbers?" Dad whispered.

Justin went numb. *Those batteries,* he thought. *Will they work?*

"Did you get the numbers?" Dad whispered urgently.

"One-four, three-five, uh . . . zero."

"Are you sure?"

"I'm sure," Justin whispered through frozen lips.

Dad pressed the power button on the transceiver.

Terror Going Down

There was a quick burst of static, which Dad muffled against his body. Justin sagged with relief. *The batteries are working,* he thought. *Thank You, Lord. I didn't run them all the way down.*

The pilot was still speaking Swahili while Dad punched Justin's numbers into the keypad. Suddenly Justin heard the pilot's tiny voice coming from the transceiver's speaker.

"What's going on?" Monique whispered into Justin's ear.

"Act natural," he whispered back.

She nodded quickly. "Look, Justin," she said aloud. "Giraffes! Three of them!"

And there they were, far below, light brown with a white web pattern all over their bodies. Still speaking into his radio, the pilot reached upward and gave a blast on the burner. Hearing the roar, the three giraffes scattered in three different directions, and several passengers chuckled.

Suddenly the pilot's voice changed from cheerful to annoyed. Justin glanced around at him and saw the man giving a worried stare in the direction of the distant elephant herd.

"Hapana," he said again and again. *"Hapana."*

Justin reached around Dad and poked Monique gently. "Do you know any Swahili at all?" he whispered.

"I think he just said 'no,'" she replied. "That's what I would say when people in the clinic wanted to know how much to pay. They would ask me, *'ngapi?'* and I would say, *'hapana.'*"

Dad leaned down between them so that their heads were close together. His transceiver was still crackling with the voices of the pilot and whomever he was talking to. The recorder's red light was still going. He pointed down over the rim at nothing in particular, and spoke in a low voice as if he were discussing something interesting below. "Keep calm, kids. I don't particularly like the mood in that guy's voice. Just keep your eyes and ears open."

"What's happening?" Monique whispered tensely. "He seems really worked up. Is he crazy?"

"Not at all," Dad said.

"Do you know how to fly a balloon?"

He gave a strained smile. "That won't be necessary. I hope."

The pilot was now almost shouting into his radio. Suddenly he snapped, *"Kwaheri!"* and pushed some buttons on the unit.

"That means 'goodbye,'" Monique whispered.

The burner gave a long, hoarse roar. Justin saw the pilot reach up and pull on a rope, and suddenly the balloon began to move sideways toward the elephant herd—and toward the dark cloud above them on the horizon, which was looking darker and angrier than ever.

"Your attention, please," the pilot said. "In a little while we will see many elephants."

The passengers made interested murmurs.

"Aren't we sort of heading into a storm?" a woman asked.

The pilot grinned, but Justin could see sweat drops on his forehead. "No. No storm. Just clouds."

"Dad," Justin whispered, "how come we're moving so fast? I didn't think balloons could be steered. I thought they just went where the wind went."

Dad swallowed nervously and glanced at the dark clouds again. "There are square holes up around the sides of the balloon. Most of the time they're covered with flaps of fabric. But when you open one of them air starts escaping, and that pushes the balloon in the opposite direction. That's what he did just now."

Justin gulped. "But if the hot air goes out, we'll fall."

Dad shook his head. "No. There's new air coming in all the time from the opening at the bottom. And the burner keeps that air hot."

The pilot's radio crackled again, and he began speaking Swahili into it.

Dad reached down and adjusted his own volume. The transceiver crackled, but they didn't hear the pilot's voice. "He changed to a different frequency," Dad said.

"Want me to try to get it again?" Justin whispered.

Dad shook his head. "That'd be too suspicious."

"Oh, *that's* what you were doing when you wandered

over there," Monique murmured. "I could try to get it this time."

"No," Dad said. "Whoever he's calling now, it's probably somebody different than he called before. And we've got bigger things to worry about right now."

Suddenly from behind them a male passenger spoke. "You know," he said loudly, "I don't think we should be moving in the direction of that weather."

The pilot broke off his radio conversation and chuckled. "Please do not worry. It will be fine."

Justin turned his head. The passenger who had spoken was a handsome middle-aged man with gray hair. His accent sounded British, but not quite. "I really disagree with you," he said. "Clouds like that can turn ugly."

"You must trust me," the pilot said. Justin saw more sweat than ever on his face. "I have been flying this balloon for several years and have never been in an accident."

"And I," said the gray-haired man, "happen to be a meteorologist with a South African weather center in Capetown."

The pilot was silent for a moment. Then he growled, "But you do not know *Kenya* weather."

"I *do* know Kenya weather. I study it and report on it all the time. I say we turn back."

"Turn back," another passenger repeated. "You've shown us some fantastic sights already."

"I cannot turn back," the pilot said obstinately. "Our support bus is already ahead of us, and lunch is almost ready there."

"Forget lunch," the gray-haired man said. "Turn back."

"I am sorry," said the pilot. He handed the man his two-way radio. "You may call my superiors if you wish. Do you speak Swahili?"

"Of course not."

"If I see there is danger," the pilot promised, "I will immediately take the balloon down."

The weatherman muttered uneasily.

"Dad," Justin whispered, "can't you do something?"

Dad shrugged. "The pilot's got a gun."

"A *gun?"*

"Shoulder holster. Under his shirt. I saw it as soon as we got on."

Monique brought her head closer. "Why?"

"It's probably useful if an animal shows up at lunchtime in the bush," Dad said. "But it would have to be a pretty big pistol to discourage a Cape buffalo."

"But why does he have it hidden?" she asked.

"So he won't scare the passengers, I suppose."

"Can't you do karate on him?" Justin asked.

"If someone subdues him, who's going to fly the balloon?" Dad asked simply. "All we can do is pray, and hope that he values his own life."

"Why does he want to get so close?" Monique said in an even lower voice.

"Not so loud," Dad whispered. "Obviously he's some kind of spotter for the poachers. They want him to get close so that he can give them details about the herd, such as how many elephants there are and which direction they're heading. Joseph Kwendo told me last night that he thinks there might be a safari balloon pilot or two who keep poachers informed."

Half an hour later they were much closer to the elephants.

"I'm cold," Monique said in her normal voice.

The gray-haired weatherman looked at her and nodded. "Of course you're cold, young lady. We're moving toward a storm system. Pilot, I really must insist that we turn back."

"We are almost there!" said the pilot in a loud, cheerful voice. "Look down below. There is our support bus, driving ahead of us. Just a few more minutes and we will have lunch. Won't that be jolly?"

No one answered him.

The pilot stared at the elephant herd for several moments in silence, then reached for his two-way radio. Dad turned away and knelt on the bench, but just as he began to fumble for his transceiver there was a powerful blast of ice-cold air. The basket began to swing crazily back and forth beneath the balloon like the pendulum on a grandfather clock. Dad nearly lost his balance, and Monique and a couple of the older women screamed. Justin instantly felt seasick.

"There now!" the gray-haired weatherman said grimly. "What did I tell you? Pilot, if you do not take this balloon down at once, I assure you that I will make a full report to your superiors and you will soon be looking for another job."

The pilot said nothing but reached up toward the ropes. Soon the balloon began to slope downward toward the small support bus, which was still throwing up dust clouds behind its wheels on the plains below. Someone inside must have been keeping an eye on the sky because the bus suddenly slowed, turned in a large circle, and came to a stop. Its doors popped open, and two men jumped out.

A couple of the passengers sighed in relief, and conversation became more relaxed. The weatherman still stared uneasily at the dark clouds, which were almost on top of them now, but Dad and Justin and Monique had fastened their eyes on the huge elephant herd that was now less than half a mile away.

"They're moving," Justin said in a low voice.

"Right," said Dad, digging in his backpack once more. "Somewhere I have a compass . . . here it is. OK. If this is north it means the herd is heading . . . northeast. Not fast, but they're definitely on the move."

Justin peered over the rim. The ground was getting close and moving quickly sideways. "We're coming down pretty fast."

"Are we going to crash?" Monique asked in alarm.

"Brace yourself," Dad said, and wedged himself into his corner and grabbed a kid in each arm.

The pilot suddenly yelped and turned on the burner full blast. Other passengers began to shout.

"Too late," Dad said tightly. "No, Justin. Don't shut your eyes. Keep alert. If we crash, go loose. Tuck and roll. If you feel ground underneath you, run like crazy."

There was a terrible thump and a loud scraping and crackling sound. Then the basket rose, the burner still roaring.

"We skipped," Dad shouted. "Now you know how a skipped rock feels."

Wham!

This time the basket hit harder, and didn't skip. The pilot, who was the only one standing, lost his balance and landed across the laps of the weatherman and a woman next to him. And then very slowly, the basket began to tip.

"Get out! Get out!" Dad shouted. "Run!"

"Shut the burner off!" roared the weatherman.

The pilot totally ignored the burner. He dove out of the tipping basket, which landed on its side and began to scrape along the ground, the sagging balloon above it dragging it along.

The next three or four seconds were the most terrifying in Justin's life. Dad's back was flat against the downward side of the basket. Some of the passengers were sprawled on top of him and others were scrambling over their backs. Justin, lying beside him, felt a heavy foot on his collarbone. Isaiah's thumb piano went *thung,* and Justin desperately put his hand over it to protect it. The burner was still roaring, and the basket still lurched and scraped across the ground.

"Fire!" screamed a distant voice. "Fire!"

Justin felt a strong arm around his waist. "Move! Move!" Dad shouted.

"Where's Monique?" he yelled.

"Move!" Dad repeated. "Run!"

Suddenly the world turned bright, hot orange. Justin felt himself picked up and carried, and then thrown. *Tuck and roll,* he heard inside his head, and curled himself into a ball. He hit the ground hard and tumbled several times.

When he stopped rolling, he struggled to a sitting position and shook his head to clear it of dizziness.

Monique. Where is Monique?

"Monique!" he shouted.

Several yards away, but frighteningly close, was the basket, still on its side. But there was no balloon. Instead, there were several bright-orange fires lying around it—burning fabric that still had traces of red, blue, and green.

"Dad! Monique!"

The weatherman was staggering toward one of the fires and, as Justin watched, he began stamping at it. A couple of other people, a man and a woman, were doing the same. Dad was nowhere in sight.

Justin scrambled to his feet. "I've got to find Monique," he repeated to himself. He began to dodge from side to side, trying to look beyond this fire and that. The heat was intense. He ran to where he could see into the basket and gasped with relief when he saw no one inside. And then on the opposite side of the basket he saw Dad, kneeling beside someone.

It was Monique.

"Monique!" Justin shouted, and ran to where his friend lay on her side on the grass. "Dad! What's wrong?"

CHAPTER 9

On TV

Dad looked up, and Justin saw that his face was covered with black ash. Part of his hair just above his right ear was burned away.

Numb, Justin knelt beside the girl, staring at her face. Her eyelids were partly open, and her eyes rolled in his direction. "Is she alive?"

"She's breathing." Dad gave a shuddery sigh. "Somebody kicked her as they went over her and knocked the wind out of her. At least I hope that's all it is."

"I'm OK," Monique said feebly.

"Stay quiet for a minute." Dad felt the side of her neck, just under her jawbone. "Your pulse is a bit slow."

A *whooshing* noise sounded behind them, and Justin turned to look. Two men in orange overalls were using fire extinguishers to put out grassfires.

"Monique," Justin said in a worried voice, "are you sure you're OK?"

She tried to roll over on one side.

"Stay down," Dad told her. "Just relax. Wiggle your toes for me. Great. Now wiggle your fingers. Excellent. That means you're not paralyzed—and you can still slug Justin when he lets loose with a knock, knock joke."

She grinned weakly. "So I've got your permission?"

"You bet." Dad rolled back on his haunches and straightened to his feet. "You can sit up, but take it easy for a few minutes. If you think something's broken let me know. And when your mom and dad get in they can take charge of you."

"I'm OK," she insisted. Glancing over at the balloon basket lying on its side, she shuddered. "That was awful. Is anybody else hurt?"

"As far as I can tell, everybody seems to be all right, thank the Lord. Just banged up a little, that's all."

Understandably, none of the crash victims was in the mood for a catered lunch on the African plains, so everybody climbed into the support bus. The pilot was one of the first to get on and sat up front beside the driver, looking straight ahead. Dad and the two kids sat in the seat behind him.

Monique poked Justin. "Look at the pilot," she said, "and then look at your dad."

"Yeah," Justin growled in a low voice. "Dad's all banged up, and his hair is burned. And the pilot looks like nothing happened."

"I saw him jump out," she said, "rather than stay with the balloon and try to turn off the burner."

Beside them, Dad was busy going through his backpack to see if everything had survived. Apparently the transceiver had made it through safely.

"What about your recorder?" Justin whispered.

"Good idea. I'd better check that too." Dad dug deeper

into the bag and finally found it. He pushed a couple of buttons on it, and suddenly a loud voice, speaking Swahili, crackled out of the speaker. Dad clapped the recorder to his chest to muffle the voice, but it was too late.

The pilot jerked his head around. His eyes locked with Dad's.

Dad quickly thumbed the recorder once more to silence it and slipped it into his shirt pocket. "How far is it to the lodge?" he asked in a friendly voice.

The other man stared at him for a few seconds more but said nothing.

"How long will it take to get there?" Justin's dad continued.

The pilot shrugged one shoulder. "One hour." He paused, as though he were going to ask another question but wasn't sure how to word it. Finally he turned to face forward again.

The trip back to the lodge wasn't quite as fun as the balloon flight had been at first. In fact, it was a whole lot bumpier. But they still saw a lot of animals. And when there was no wildlife to watch, Justin tried to plunk out "Green Fields of Grace" on the thumb piano while listening to Shannon's voice in his mind.

"Monique, no," Dad said earnestly. "Don't do that."

Justin glanced around. Monique's head was resting against Dad's arm. "Dad, she's trying to get some sleep."

"I'm tired," she said. "Just a quick nap?"

"No you don't," Dad said to her. "There's a slight chance you might have a concussion, and I want to make sure you stay alert, at least until your folks get a chance to look you over. Justin, tell her a joke. Make her mad."

Monique grinned sleepily. "That'll send me into a coma for sure," she said, and sat up straight. "But remember, I'm not paralyzed, so that means I can slug you."

The pilot was right. The trip back to the lodge took about an hour. And as they jounced toward the parking lot, Dad gave a low whistle.

"Whoa," he said, "news travels fast, even in Africa."

A small single-engine plane was parked by the side of the main road, while near the front door of the lodge, directly in their path, stood a Kenyan man and woman. The man supported a large TV camera on his shoulder, while the woman held a microphone and a clipboard.

The bus driver glanced at the balloon pilot and said something under his breath. The pilot spat out a few syllables that sounded like Swahili swearing. Stepping on the brakes, the driver brought the bus to a temporary stop, and the pilot jumped out and started jogging toward some side buildings, while the bus picked up speed again.

"This is the pits," Monique moaned. "We're gonna be on TV." She brushed at her clothes and half stood, trying to see her reflection in the bus's rearview mirror.

Justin stared at the back of the retreating pilot and scowled. "Look at that coward run," he snarled. "I hope they fire him. And I hope he never gets a job anywhere else again."

"Hey, don't go saying anything like that about him in front of the camera," Dad said in a low voice. "He's probably just as much a hero as a villain. This could have been a whole lot worse. We've all done things we weren't proud of, haven't we? Things that were dumb, and maybe even dangerous to other people. Right?"

Justin's stomach lurched as he suddenly remembered the transceiver batteries.

"Let's cut him a little slack," Dad insisted. "Show him a little grace. Hey, look at that!"

Justin and Monique sat up alertly. "What?"

"Joseph Kwendo's standing there with the TV people!"

"All right!" Monique said excitedly. "Maybe he's got news of Isaiah."

The bus pulled to a stop. One by one the passengers stepped off. Justin noticed that several were limping. The female reporter was saying, "Sir? Madam? May I ask a question? How are you feeling? Are you hurt? What was it like?"

When Monique and Justin stepped off the bus, the woman spotted them. "Stay with me," she called to the cameraman. "Stay tight. Young lady, are you hurt?"

Monique shook her head.

"How are you feeling?"

"A little sore." Monique edged sideways.

"What happened?"

"Um, we got close to a storm, and—"

Dad's smiling voice suddenly said, "Sorry, these young people have been through a lot. We were all very fortunate."

With a grateful smile at him, Monique escaped the camera and joined Justin. Together they hurried to where Joseph Kwendo was standing.

"Mr. Kwendo!" Justin said. "Have you heard from Isaiah?"

The ranger glanced uneasily at the TV people and beckoned them aside. "I have told them about the poachers," he said, "but not about my son. I would prefer that they not know." He noticed the twosome's mussed clothing. His eyes widened. "What exactly happened?"

They quickly gave the man a report. Monique said, "We can't understand why the pilot got so close to the storm. But Mr. Case said he was probably a spotter for the poachers."

Mr. Kwendo nodded. "And not only that." He glanced over toward the TV crew, and as he did so Dad made a final comment to the reporter and turned away. Catching sight of Mr. Kwendo, he walked quickly toward him.

"Joseph. What's the latest? Did you find your boy?"

Mr. Kwendo shook his head. "I have bad news, and there is not much time."

"Bad news?" Justin said anxiously. "Is Isaiah all right?"

The ranger turned both his palms helplessly skyward. "I do not know."

"Where is he?" Monique asked.

"I do not know that either. But we must move quickly."

"Kids," Dad said, fumbling in his wallet, "get lunch there in that restaurant. You're probably about dead from hunger, right? Don't drink the water unless it's bottled water. Then get up to our suite. Go."

Soon Justin found himself sitting at a tiny table by a window overlooking the African plains, with Monique across from him. Both were silent for a long time, energetically eating what they'd ordered, including lots of french fries and a superb sauce to dip them in. But finally Justin looked up.

"Monique."

"What?"

"Tell you something if you won't tell Dad."

She eyed him suspiciously. "Is it a joke?"

"No."

"I never repeat your jokes anyway, so you don't have to worry."

Justin hunched his chair closer to the little table. Isaiah's thumb piano clunked musically against the edge.

"Wow, you're still wearing that," Monique said. "Did it come through the crash okay?"

Justin plunked out part of a melody. "Sounds fine."

"What's that song? I remember it vaguely."

"'Green Fields of Grace.' But don't interrupt me. I've gotta tell you something."

"You're serious? It isn't one of your jokes?"

He shook his head.

"Well, go ahead."

He quickly told her about when he was homesick and worried about Isaiah and how he'd "borrowed" Dad's transceiver batteries to listen to Shannon Fagin. "And I think," he said, "that I went to sleep while the CD player was still running."

She gasped. *"No."*

"I did. When I woke up the disk was still spinning."

Monique glanced far out across the plains to where their balloon had hovered. "And yet your dad still had enough battery power to listen in on what that pilot was saying."

Justin nodded.

"You'd better say a thank-You prayer," she said.

"I will. I *did.*"

"And tell your dad."

Justin winced. "I think I'll just get the batteries charged up and not tell him."

Monique frowned at him. "Tell him."

"Monique!"

"Tell him."

Justin slid out of the booth. "OK. Sometime," he added under his breath.

Justin paid for the meal, and they dashed upstairs to the suite. Joseph Kwendo was speaking to someone on the telephone, and Dad was snapping a suitcase shut.

"Got your gas tanks filled?" he asked. "Good. You're going to need it. By the way, Monique, Joseph Kwendo just told me that your parents are here."

"Mom and Dad? *Where?*"

"Their suite's down the hall, two doors on the right. They got here when we were on the balloon flight. They've just come in from doing a bit of exploring in the Land Rover. Go say hi to them. And by the way, we're heading out in five minutes."

CHAPTER 10

Search Party

Monique looked bewildered, but darted off.

"Heading out?" Justin asked. "Where?"

"I'll tell you on the way. Just get packed. Pack for overnight, Justin. And pack tight—there's not a lot of room in the Land Rover."

"OK."

Joseph Kwendo, who had just hung up the telephone, heard the last little bit of their conversation. "Your name is Justin?" he asked.

Justin nodded, knowing what was coming.

"And your last name is Case?"

Justin nodded again.

Joseph Kwendo's worried face relaxed for a moment into a strained smile. "Very interesting. That makes your full name Justin Case."

Justin nodded. "Uh-huh."

" 'Just in case,' " the ranger explained helpfully.

Dad chuckled. "It's the cross my son has to bear. He's named after a beloved relative of my wife's. He can thank his lucky stars that his first name isn't Court or Pencil. Or Suit. Speaking of suitcase, get packing, my son."

No chance to charge those four double-A's, Justin thought

as he crammed underwear and socks and other things into his backpack. He glanced at his CD player. *If Dad would've brought along a decent supply of batteries, I could take that along.* "We're coming back here, right?" he asked aloud.

"Yes, but don't leave anything of value in the room."

"OK." Justin fitted the dead CD player into his belt pack. "I'm set."

"Run down the hall and tell the Walters we're ready."

A couple of minutes later Justin was jogging down the hall behind Monique as they headed outdoors. "What's happening?" he asked. "Where are we going?"

"I don't know, but we'll find out in the Land Rover."

"Who's coming along?"

"Everybody except Mr. Kwendo," she said over her shoulder.

The seven-passenger Land Rover was already purring, with Jerry Walters at the wheel. Monique and Justin slid into the back, and Lucinda Walters joined them. Dad sat up front beside Dr. Walters.

As the Land Rover began to move, questions got answered.

"Where are we going?" Justin asked.

"To the elephant herd," Dad answered. "We're going to find Isaiah and his cousins—if we can."

"How are we going to find them? And what about that storm?"

Dad gestured toward the east. "It's fizzled out, I think."

Monique leaned forward. "And where's Mr. Kwendo?"

Dad jerked his thumb toward the roof. "Up there. In the

TV station's plane. Or he will be in an hour. He's going to be our spotter as we look for the poacher lookouts."

"I thought we were looking for Isaiah," she said.

Dad turned and looked at her. "We are."

"He's not a poacher lookout!" she protested.

"Guess what," Dad said. "He is."

"How do we know that?" Justin asked indignantly.

"While you two were eating in the restaurant Joseph filled me in. It turns out that the owner of Ship of the Desert Camel Racing is also involved in a major poaching ring."

"The man we saw in the train?" Monique asked.

"The man you saw in the train. Kwendo contacted the Nairobi police, and they arrested another of the Ship of the Desert guys, and he talked. He said that the boss was heading here and that he'd just picked up three kids as lookouts. He and the kids had headed west on the train, and their plan was to be in place late last night or early this morning."

"Picked them up?" Justin asked. "Kidnapped them?"

"Or sweet-talked them into making a bit of money," Dad said.

"So Isaiah is a poacher?" Suddenly the thumb piano around Justin's neck hung heavy. "Isaiah's out there helping people kill elephants so they can saw off their tusks?"

Monique patted Justin on the shoulder. "Remember what he was always talking about?"

Justin nodded glumly. "Mon-nee." He slipped the thumb piano's thong off his neck and tossed it into the far back of the Land Rover. It made a musical mournful *clunk*.

"Robert?" said Dr. Walters. "Am I going the right direction?"

"See that low mountain on the horizon? Joseph and I figured that we should head straight in that direction for one hour. By the way," Dad said gratefully, "he owes you big-time. You too, Lucinda. You're putting your family safari on hold and you're using your Land Rover to help find his relatives."

"That's not a problem," said Lucinda Walters, speaking for the first time. "But isn't this fairly dangerous?"

"You mean because of the animals?"

She nodded. "Because of that, partly. Here we are, out in the bush with no guide."

"Kind of," Dad admitted. "But Kwendo's going to guide us, in a way. He's staying behind at the lodge for a bit, phoning for additional ranger support. But then when he thinks we're getting close to the herd, he'll come overhead in the TV plane."

"So the TV plane was how he got here in the first place?" Monique asked.

"Yes. He called the station and promised them first chance at a breaking major story, and they instantly said yes." Dad unclipped the transceiver from his belt and thumbed the power button. A brief crackle of static sounded, and he thumbed the button again, turning it off. "We're going to keep radio silence for"—he glanced at his watch—"47 more minutes. And then Joseph will fly over and we'll touch base."

"I don't like this," Mrs. Walters said.

"How come, Mom?" her daughter asked.

"How can we possibly find three boys in these millions of acres?"

"She's got a point, Robert," Jerry Walters said. "It's not like they're going to be strolling down a country road in plain sight. The poachers will have them under cover."

"It's not really all that hard," Dad said comfortingly. "The first thing is to find the elephant herd, and we've done that. The second thing is to figure out which way that herd is moving, and we've done that. From the balloon it seemed to me they were heading northeast. And Joseph will confirm that from the plane."

"But won't the poachers spot the plane and get suspicious?" Justin asked.

"It's not an official plane. The station chartered it at the airport."

"I understand now," Dr. Walters said. "If you can predict the future path of the herd, you've got a good chance of finding the poachers."

"Right," Dad said. "We know they're close, otherwise the balloon pilot wouldn't have been taking the risk of radioing the elephants' movements. And we're not talking just three or four poachers. There'll probably be dozens—several groups of them, all waiting with their rifles and chainsaws."

"So that's what the pilot was doing?" Justin asked. "Telling the poachers which way the elephants were moving?"

"And maybe more."

Justin and Monique looked at him, puzzled.

"Joseph thinks the balloon pilot wanted to get close

enough so he could scare the elephants with the sound of the burner."

Jerry Walters glanced at Dad. "Sort of herd them along, you mean? Would that work?"

His daughter nodded. "It worked with giraffes."

"My worry," Mrs. Walters said, "is that those boys will be trampled."

Dad nodded. "It's always a possibility. Let's just keep them in our prayers."

Forty minutes later, as they rounded a line of trees, Dr. Walters gasped. "Lucinda, look. I have never seen anything like this in my life. Monique, *look* at that." They saw a breathtakingly long line of dark-gray beasts, ears slowly flapping, and trunks swinging from side to side.

This isn't a zoo, Justin thought with a sudden shock of fear. *There aren't any fences, and Isaiah's out there somewhere. And he doesn't even have a Land Rover to protect him.*

"It's getting dark," Justin said aloud.

"Sundown's about 5:30," Dr. Walters commented.

"Come on, Joseph, get airborne," Dad murmured, craning his neck to search the sky. Then he glanced at the herd and chuckled. "Aren't they amazing? We saw them from the balloon this morning."

"There are hundreds of them," Mrs. Walters said in a voice of awe.

Her husband shuddered. "Those poor boys," he said. "I wouldn't be outside here at night for any amount of money."

Mr. Case took out a small pair of binoculars and turned

to search the sky behind him. "Joseph should be airborne now. Whoa."

"What?" Justin asked nervously.

"We definitely won't have a lot of daylight to work with. It's probably going to be an overnighter."

"We're ready," said Jerry Walters.

"Got a rifle?" Mr. Case asked.

"No."

"No rifle?"

Dr. Walters shrugged. "Remember, this was going to be an ordinary safari. With a guide. The guide would have had the rifle."

"Well," Dad said, "I'm sure glad Joseph Kwendo is going to be buzzing around overhead. But once he has to go back to the lodge we're on our own." He unclipped the transceiver from his belt and began beeping numbers into its keypad. "Joseph? Can you hear me?"

Monique took hold of Justin's wrist and began to squeeze.

"Monique?" Mrs. Walters said. "Are you feeling all right?"

Her daughter hastily snatched her hand away. "I'm OK, Mom."

"Don't be frightened."

"I'm not."

Justin's stomach had turned to ice. *Dear Jesus, charge those batteries. Please.*

The transceiver crackled.

"Joseph," Dad said again. "Come in, Joseph."

"This is Joseph. Is this Robert?"

Justin breathed a shuddery prayer of thanks. His eyes slid sideways and met Monique's.

"This is Robert. I know we need to keep transmissions short. Can you see us?"

"Not yet."

"Can you see the herd?"

"Yes, I have the herd in sight."

"We are—" Dad broke off and glanced at the Land Rover's built-in compass—"due west, probably a quarter mile." He scanned the skies to the southwest. "I see you now."

"Drive due north and parallel to the herd. I'll keep looking for you. Contact me again in two minutes."

"This is not going to work," Mrs. Walters said. "Are the poachers going to actually try to shoot the elephants in daylight? With an airplane flying overhead?"

Dad set a timer on his wristwatch. "Remember," he reminded her, "we don't have to concentrate on the poachers. We're hunting for lookouts. And," he said, looking around soberly at them all, "we've *got* to find them."

"Tonight, you mean?" Justin said.

Dad nodded. "If possible."

"Why tonight?"

His father sighed. "Because of something Joseph told me. And it's not nice."

Justin licked his lips, which were dry. "What?"

"It's the way the poachers treat the lookouts. I didn't want to tell you this, but I'd better tell you now."

"How?" Monique asked. "How do they treat them?"

"A lookout," Dad explained, "keeps an eye out for park

rangers, or for safari tourists who seem to be too nosy. They signal the poachers if they spot anything. And once the poachers spot the signal they decide whether to hide or run."

His watch alarm began to beep, and he picked up the transceiver. "Come in, Joseph."

"I have you in sight," Joseph Kwendo's voice said.

Dad peered out the window. "I see you too. What should we do?"

"Keep traveling due north. I will not be talking to you unless I see something you should examine. Just keep your radio on. How are your batteries?"

Monique and Justin glanced at each other. Justin's stomach froze again.

"Fine, fine," Dad said. "Don't worry about us. By the way, could you use the 360-degree reference when you want us to go somewhere? Straight ahead is zero, right is 90 degrees, and so on."

"I will do that. Continue traveling at zero degrees. You are traveling faster than the herd. Go a mile ahead of them and get close to their path."

Dad turned around to face the others again. "Like I said, when the poachers get the signal from the lookouts, they decide whether or not to run." He cleared his throat nervously. "And once in a while they go back and pick up the lookouts. But most often they don't."

Monique gasped. "They don't?"

"That's what Joseph told me."

"They just leave the lookouts out there alone, with the animals?"

Dad nodded. "If a lookout is lucky, he'll get a ride with whoever it was he saw coming. If it's a ranger, and if the ranger thinks he's a lookout, he'll go to jail until trial. At least he's safe. But the lookouts that are abandoned . . ." He let his voice trail off.

Mrs. Walters put her hand to Justin's forehead. "Are you ill?" she asked him. "You're coming down with something, aren't you?"

He shook his head, and turned away from her as though he were watching for the plane.

"Are you sure?"

"I'm fine, Mrs. Walters."

"Monique, what about you? You two seem so quiet."

"Mom, we're worried about Isaiah."

"I can imagine," she said.

Dad's transceiver crackled. "Come in, Joseph."

"I've spotted something."

Dad sat forward alertly. "Give me a direction, in degrees. We're still heading north at zero."

The transceiver gurgled and hissed and then went silent. Monique grabbed hold of Justin's arm and held on tightly.

"Joseph," Dad said, "please repeat. You're garbled."

This time the transceiver gargled even more faintly.

And then it went dead.

"Don't do that," said Dad, shaking the transceiver. "Don't die on me." He rolled down the Land Rover window and held the unit's antenna outside. "Joseph!" he shouted. "Repeat!"

Nothing.

In the back seat, Justin put his head in his palms.

CHAPTER 11

Pointed Danger

Mrs. Walters tried to put her arm around him, but he wouldn't sit up. His face, covered with his hands, was almost down between his knees.

"Justin," she said softly. "Don't feel bad. We're doing what we can. The Lord can see where Isaiah is."

He shook his head violently. "It's *my* fault!"

During the four seconds of puzzled silence that followed his remark, everyone heard the drone of a single-engine airplane high in the sky.

"It's not your fault," Lucinda Walters said gently. "Those three boys made their own decisions, and—"

"No!" Justin's words were blurry through his hands. "The batteries! I used the batteries!"

"What batteries?" she asked him gently.

"The transceiver batteries! For the CD player!"

Justin began weeping. He wept and wept and wept, and tried to slide off the seat away from Mrs. Walters.

"Oh, my son," Dad said in a thick, fuzzy voice. "Oh, my son."

"And now," Justin gulped, "Isaiah's going to die."

"He won't die," Monique said softly.

"Yes he will! And it'll be all my fault."

"Justin," Dad said. "Justin, listen. Stop crying. Get a grip. Give me some facts. You used these batteries for the CD player. How many times?"

Justin sat up and sniffed loudly. "Two times."

"That shouldn't have burned them down this far."

"But the second time I went to sleep and let it play all night."

Dad let out his breath in a long sigh. "Aha. OK, does anybody have anything along with them that uses double-A's? Monique, do you have a radio or something? Jerry, an electric razor?"

They all shook their heads.

"Does the Land Rover have its own CB radio or anything like that?"

Jerry Walters shook his head miserably.

Dad glanced at his watch. "We've got an hour of daylight. We'd better use it wisely. Do we have something to signal Joseph with? Anybody have a mirror?"

Dr. Walters pulled the Land Rover to a stop. Then he took a Swiss knife off his belt, opened a blade, and began to work on the screws behind the vehicle's rearview mirror.

Soon Dad was standing outside the Land Rover, doing his best to reflect the late-afternoon sun toward the plane. "Got him!" he finally said through the open windows. "He waggled his wings at us. By now he's probably figured out that our radio's down. Now he's turning. He's heading back toward the lodge."

"Why doesn't he land?" Monique asked.

"On this kind of terrain that's called 'suicide,'" Dad

said. "He's heading back home. He knows our position and he's going to—well, I'm not sure what he's going to do."

"Dad," Justin called out in a voice weak from crying.

Dad came to the window and looked inside. "What?" he asked gently.

"Isaiah knows what the Land Rover looks like."

Dad raised his eyebrows. "Monique, is that true?"

"Yes," she said. "He came by the shantytown quite a lot on his way to work."

"Did he ever talk about it?"

She shrugged. "Not really, but he knew it was there. One time he asked me how much it cost."

Lucinda Walters put her arm around Justin. "So what you're saying," she told him, "is that if Isaiah saw the Land Rover he might recognize it and try to see what our problem might be."

"Maybe," Dr. Walters put in, "but then again, maybe not. I mean, if you're a poacher's lookout you're going to be careful, especially in his situation. And he might not be close enough to get a good look."

"He'd have binoculars," Dad commented. "The poachers would give them binoculars to help them be better lookouts."

"But even so—" Dr. Walters was going to continue, but Justin's muffled voice interrupted him.

"The thumb piano, Dad."

Dad leaned in through the window and stared at his son. "The thumb piano? What are you going to do, hold it out the window and play it?"

Justin shook his head. "Tie it to the antenna and drive around."

Dad's face froze in thought. Then he smiled. "Can't hurt. Where is it?"

"Back here." Justin put his knees on the back seat and leaned over and rummaged among the luggage and sleeping bags. A musical *thunk* sounded, and he pulled the item out.

"Whoa, bright-red," said Dad. "Are you OK with giving this a try, Jerry?"

"By all means."

Justin wriggled through his window, sat on the lower part of it, and carefully tied the thumb piano to the antenna.

"Problem," Monique said suddenly.

"What?" Justin asked her.

"We can't drive around."

"Why not?"

"We'll get lost."

"Maybe," Dad said thoughtfully.

"Couldn't we just call out Isaiah's name?" Monique suggested.

Her father glanced at the slanting sun. "Get in," he said firmly, starting the engine. "Let's drive. Everybody keep your eyes open."

"You sure, Jerry?" Dad asked.

"Let's do it."

"I'll get out my scope," Justin said, fumbling in his backpack and fishing around under his dead CD player.

"This is like looking for a needle in a haystack," Mrs.

Walters said. "And it's not like Isaiah wants to be found."

"It's all we can do," her husband reminded her.

He drove slowly along, sometimes criss-crossing ahead of the elephant herd and sometimes ranging to either side of it.

"It's been a half hour," Lucinda Walters said. "We've seen nobody."

"OK, kids," Dad said. "Start yelling Isaiah's name. Monique, you take the right side, Justin the left."

"Isaiah!" they screamed into the sunset. "Isaiah! Isaiah!"

And then, while they rested their voices, Dad called. Then the Walters. Then the young people again.

"The herd's stopping," Dr. Walters said, squinting at them through the deepening twilight. "Probably bedding down for the night."

"Head for that clear space," Dad said. "I'd rather be out in the open so we can be seen in the moonlight."

Dr. Walters turned the Land Rover in the direction Dad was pointing.

"What's that?" Monique suddenly asked.

Justin peered ahead. "Where?"

"That big black mound. Is that dirt?"

Dr. Walters turned so that the headlights shone in that direction.

"Oh, no," Dad said, "what a tragedy."

"It's an elephant," said Lucinda Walters in a wondering voice. "Is it dead? Sleeping?"

"Look at the tusks," her husband said simply.

There were no tusks. Just white stumps gleaming in the headlights.

How long they sat there watching the elephant nobody really knew. It was Justin who broke the spell.

"There's something moving out there," he said.

"Where?" Dad asked.

"Just to the right of the elephant. Farther out."

"Your young eyes are better than my old ones. I can't see it."

"I can," Monique said. "It's like a bull. With horns."

"Whoa, Jerry," Dad said quickly. "Keep that engine running."

Dr. Walters took a quick breath. "Cape buffalo," he gasped. "The most dangerous animal in Kenya."

"You're not kidding," Dad said.

Lucinda Walters said, "Are you sure? I would have said lions were the most dangerous."

"When they're in a herd, Cape buffalo aren't as dangerous," Justin said. "That's what the balloon pilot said. But if you have just one or two of them alone, they could attack people."

"And," Monique said, as if she were giving a report at school, "Cape buffalo kill more people in Kenya than lions or elephants do."

"Turn off the headlights, Jerry," Dad suggested. "It might charge."

And it was while they were nervously watching the Cape buffalo in the gathering gloom that two terrifying things happened.

The first was that the buffalo began pawing the ground and moving forward.

The second was a thundering thumping on the back windows of the Land Rover.

CHAPTER 12

Grace Abundant

Monique and her mother screamed.

Justin shouted in terror.

Dr. Walters panicked, started the engine, and turned on the headlights.

Something with eyes pressed its face against Justin's window, and it was shouting too.

But then he saw who it was.

And Monique saw too. "Isaiah!" she shrieked. "Let him in, Justin!"

Justin pushed the door open, and Isaiah was on his lap, sobbing wildly. "Malcolm! Kenton! They are still out there!" he babbled. A huge pair of old binoculars dangled from his neck.

More thumping sounded on the windows, and Monique opened the other door. Isaiah's two frightened cousins crowded in, stepping on feet and begging that the doors be shut.

"Why did you keep moving so fast?" Isaiah gasped to Justin and the others. "I saw the Land Rover in my binoculars and thought I recognized it. Then I saw my thumb piano, and we've been racing after you ever since."

A hoarse bellow sounded one buffalo-length away from

the Land Rover's headlights. Everybody stopped what they were doing or saying and stared uncertainly at the dark-skinned animal. Above each of its tiny eyes were two wrinkles, and above the wrinkles its horns began, curling outward and then up and in again, ending with sharp points.

"Back off, Jerry," Dad said tensely.

Dr. Walters shifted into reverse and began a slow retreat. The buffalo bellowed hoarsely and advanced.

"It wouldn't attack a Land Rover, would it?" Monique asked.

"Yes," Kenton said, "it will attack. You must shoot it."

"We don't have a gun," Dr. Walters said.

"Then drive away, very quickly!"

Dr. Walters paused. And while he paused the buffalo lunged forward, ramming his horns into the front of the Land Rover, bending the hood.

"Get out of here, Jerry!" Dad said. "Don't let him get a headlight."

Suddenly from just above them there was the brief snarl of a powerful engine, and for just an instant the disappearing tail of a climbing airplane could be seen.

"It's Mr. Kwendo!" Monique shouted.

"Good news!" Dad said, breathing a great sigh of relief. "He must have been circling up there. Then he saw our headlights, and now he knows where we are."

The buffalo turned to watch the plane disappear. Jerry Walters wrestled with the shift lever and stepped on the accelerator pedal. The Land Rover leaped forward and pushed the animal, which bellowed again and retreated.

"No! No!" the cousins shouted. "You will make it angry!"

"Stay close to it, Jerry," Dad commanded. "Don't let the buffalo back far enough away to charge us again."

But the mighty beast swerved quickly to the right, too quickly for the Land Rover to follow. Out of the darkness it charged again, ramming the front door and splintering the window.

Jerry Walters backed rapidly and soon had the buffalo in his headlights again.

The animal stood still for a moment, as though thinking. Its huge hoofs pawed the ground. And then it lowered its head.

Monique screamed.

But at that moment the sound of an airplane could be heard in the distance. The Cape buffalo paused as the sound grew louder. Then suddenly the noise grew so ear-shattering that the massive animal made an abrupt turn, seeking retreat from the unknown threat.

"The return of Joseph Kwendo," Mr. Case said, watching the plane disappear in the distance.

Just then a set of headlights loomed up on Justin's side of the Land Rover, and doors slammed. Two men in park ranger uniforms peered curiously in through the windows.

* * *

"Dad?"

It was 3:00 in the morning, but nobody was sleepy. The rangers had led the banged-up Land Rover by the quickest and safest route back to the lodge. Now everyone, including Mr. Kwendo, was sitting in the Cases' suite drinking hot chocolate from the lodge's kitchen.

"Dad," Justin said again, "will you forgive me?"

Robert Case smiled at his son. "You mean about the batteries? Of course I forgive you."

"I'm sorry I disobeyed you." Justin looked down. "I mean, we could have been killed."

"That's true. If Mr. Kwendo hadn't buzzed that Cape buffalo, I don't know what would have happened to us."

Joseph Kwendo spoke. "The Cape buffalo is a deadly beast. And with that dead elephant lying there the lions might have shown up sooner or later."

"I got us into a lot of trouble," Justin continued. "I just wish there was something I could do to make up for it."

Dad chuckled. "You could tell us what's so great about Sally Ferguson that would make you borrow my transceiver batteries to listen to her CD."

"Shannon Fagin," Monique corrected helpfully.

Justin blushed. "It's partly this one song she sings."

"Well, what song is it?"

"'Green Fields of Grace.'"

Lucinda Walters said, "That's a beautiful title. How do the lyrics go?"

"Sing it, Justin," Monique said.

He stared at her as though she'd lost her mind. "I'm not gonna sing it."

"Well then, tell us the words," Mrs. Walters said, "if you remember them."

He paused. "I'll try," he finally said. "It's supposed to be God talking to us."

Let Me take you from this place,
Far away from steel and steam,
Far away from smoky towers,
To My soft, green fields of grace.

Let Me free you from your fears,
Come away from dark and danger,
Come away from guilt and shame,
Come and let me dry your tears,
In My soft, green fields of grace.

Justin paused, and took a deep breath. "This next one is kind of—" He broke off, and went on in a trembly voice.

I don't care how bad you've been,
Who you've hurt and how you've wandered,
Come away from fear and anger,
Come and let Me dry your tears,
In My soft, green fields of grace.

By the time he was done, Monique was crying softly. Isaiah sniffed a couple of times. Malcolm and Kenton were staring, expressionless, at the floor.

Isaiah's fingers brushed the metal notes of his red thumb piano. "I'm sorry too, *baba,*" he said.

Joseph Kwendo's face did not change. He said, "And

what are you sorry for, my son?"

"I'm sorry for coming here on the train. At first I thought we were going to earn some money helping set up camel races."

"So did we," Malcolm said. "But I started to get suspicious when Mr. Ocholla told us not to come near him on the train, to pretend we did not know him. Finally I went to his car to talk to him, and he got really angry. That's when he told me we would be lookouts."

"And then they gave us each binoculars and a mirror," Kenton said.

"To signal with, if we saw something," Malcolm explained. "And we knew that the balloon pilot was a spotter and lookout of sorts too, but when we saw the fire we wondered if something had gone wrong."

"Well, I'm thankful it's turned out all right," Dad said, "thanks to the grace of God."

Mr. Kwendo smiled wearily. "I do forgive you, Isaiah. Thank God you were spared."

When everyone had left the Case suite and Monique had gone to bed in her room, Dad turned on his laptop.

"I'm still a little keyed up," he told his son. "I'm going to see if I can get through to the international number for our e-mail. Whoa," he said a few minutes later. "You're in for another adventure."

"I'm too tired," Justin said in a sleepy voice from his bed. "I don't want to go."

"You've gotta go. I'm going to be out of town, so you're going to have to stay with your mom wherever she goes."

"Where's that?"

"Thanks to her dedicated volunteer work in the school cafeteria, she has won airline tickets for two to the Vitality Vegetarian Foods Corporation's open house."

"Oh, Dad," Justin wailed sleepily, "do I *have* to?"

"Sorry, pal."

"It'll be boring."

"That's what you said before you got mixed up in that crystal dragon adventure in Seattle."

"I know, but—"

Dad grinned and snapped the laptop shut. "There's probably all sorts of danger you don't know about in the vegetarian food business. International criminals, wild screams in the night, car chases, that kind of thing."

Well, it wasn't quite like that, but as Justin and his two new friends would discover, there would be three times the adventure—and fun—they thought there would be.

The next morning everybody gathered for worship in Justin's room before going their separate ways. Isaiah was curious about the Shannon Fagin song.

"What is grace?" Isaiah asked. "I always thought it was a prayer before a meal."

"I once heard a definition I thought was really clear," Lucinda Walters commented. "'Grace is kindness you don't deserve.'"

Justin nodded quickly. "I like that," he said. "That's what Dad and the rest of you gave me last night. I disobeyed Dad and burned the batteries down, and that put us all in danger. But you forgave me."

Isaiah glanced at his father, who gazed at him with a small smile. "And *you* forgave *me, baba,"* he said.

Dad reached for his Bible. "But the best grace of all," he said, "is the grace God gives to us—the kindness we don't deserve. Let me read you a few verses that show how this works." (Fill in the blanks in the following verses. Mr. Case is using the New International Version.)

Deuteronomy 7:7, 8: "The Lord did not set his affection on you and ________ you because you were more ________ than other peoples, for you were the ________ of all peoples. But it was because the Lord ________ you. . . ."

Romans 3:23, 24: "For all have ________ and fall short of the ________ of God, and are ________ freely by his ________ through the redemption that came by Christ Jesus."

Romans 5:6-8: "You see, at just the right time, when we were still ________, Christ died for the ________. Very rarely will anyone die for a ________ man, though for a good man someone might possibly dare to die. But God ________ his own love for us in this: While we were still ________ , Christ died for us."

Ephesians 2:8, 9: "For it is by ________ you have been saved, through ________—and this not from yourselves, it is the ________ of God—not by works, so that no one can ________ ."

1 Timothy 1:15, 16: "Here is a ________ saying that deserves full acceptance: Christ Jesus came into the world to ________ ________—of whom I am the ________. But for that very reason I was shown ________ so that in me, the worst of sinners, Christ Jesus might display his unlimited ________ as an example for those who would ________ on him and receive eternal life."